Praise for Ca[x

"I loved getting to know Cady! When I owned Falling Rock Cafe and Bookstore in Munising, MI, we sold many copies of Ann Dallman's first book in this series, *Cady and the Bear Necklace*. It was definitely a favorite among our customers. The mystery component of this second book kept me turning the pages, and I loved the coming-of-age aspects as well. It is very hard to find books for this age group about Native American culture, so I was happy to see another book by such an excellent writer and wonderful storyteller! Young people will enjoy the diverse themes, including journal writing, reservation life, Native American artistry and intergenerational relationships. I hope there is a book 3 in this series!"

Nancy Dwyer, Munising, MI

"*Cady and the Birchbark Box* is a wonderful second addition to the series. It is refreshing to read a book you can identify with and that represents your people and community - especially when there were so few fiction works involving the Anishnaabe people from the Upper Peninsula. Ms. Dallman provided many historically and culturally accurate examples that will encourage youth to keep reading. As an adult, it was a strong reminder to follow the traditions we were taught - no matter where you end up in life.

- Cassie Gill, tribal member of Hannahville Potawatomi and former high school student of Ms. Dallman

"I was away at a wholesale show when the books arrived; I just unpacked them today. I was able to read *Cady and the Bear Necklace* while sitting in our booth waiting for customers. I loved it! I really liked how the Native American traditions and modern way of life was interspersed throughout the book and never felt like it was part of a "lecture," which I find often in YA. Well done!"

Laurie Rose, owner, Thunder Bay Press, West Branch, MI

"Ann Dallman's writing is a teacher's dream come true. Cady is a character students can relate to and learn from. While Cady is learning about her Native American culture and traditions, readers become immersed in a culture they may not have knowledge of. The Cady Whirlwind Thunder series is great for teachers who are looking for read-alouds that provide an opportunity to introduce new vocabulary and language skills. Ann's career as an English teacher shines through in her books."

Gina Zanon, 5th-grade teacher, Menominee, MI

"Cady Whirlwind Thunder has a name befitting her delightful, whirlwind personality. This beautiful short novel presents an intriguing mystery woven with Cady's Native American heritage and cultural reverence for birchbark. I smiled many times at Cady's problems and family challenges. Cady has a sense of humor regarding teenage struggles and good advice on topics ranging from not talking back to her parents to finding ways to get along with gnarly friends. The reverence for her grandmothers will also create a warm spot in a reader's heart. This well-crafted novel immerses readers in the elegance of Native American culture, as it delivers an emotional, intriguing mystery that readers from middle grade through adults will enjoy. Highly recommended!"

Christine DeSmet, author, *Fudge Shop* mystery series and member, *Mystery Writers of America* and *Sisters in Crime*

"I like the open school with a diverse population and rural setting in the Cady Whirlwind Thunder mysteries. Readers will learn cultural information, such as how important elders are, while enjoying the story. The mystery now is *what will the mystery be*! We want to know... the blue jay seems to know. Cady is respectful, a role model and anything but boring."

Carolyn Wilhelm, *Midwest Book Review*

Cady and
The Birchbark Box

A Cady Whirlwind Thunder Mystery

Ann Dallman

Modern History Press

Ann Arbor, MI

Cady and the Birchbark Box: A Cady Whirlwind Thunder Mystery

Cover art by Haley Greenfeather English

Interior illustrations by Joanna Walitalo

Book #2 in the Cady Whirlwind Thunder Mysteries

Library of Congress Cataloging-in-Publication Data
Names: Dallman, Ann, author.
Title: Cady and the birchbark box / by Ann Dallman.
Description: Ann Arbor, MI : Modern History Press, 2022. | Series: Cady
  Whirlwind Thunder mysteries ; 2 | Audience: Ages 10-12. | Audience:
  Grades 4-6. | Summary: "Cady is tasked with solving the mystery of a
  birchbark box containing an old journal and helping clear the name of a
  deceased tribe member"-- Provided by publisher.
Identifiers: LCCN 2022003400 (print) | LCCN 2022003401 (ebook) | ISBN
  9781615996513 (paperback) | ISBN 9781615996520 (hardcover) | ISBN
  9781615996537 (eBook)
Subjects: CYAC: Shipwrecks--Fiction. | Potawatomi Indians--Fiction. |
  Indians of North America--Michigan--Fiction. | Schools--Fiction. | Upper
  Peninsula (Mich.)--Fiction. | Mystery and detective stories. | LCGFT:
  Novels. | Novels. | Detective and mystery fiction.
Classification: LCC PZ7.1.D2873 Cag 2022 (print) | LCC PZ7.1.D2873
  (ebook) | DDC [Fic]--dc23
LC record available at https://lccn.loc.gov/2022003400
LC ebook record available at https://lccn.loc.gov/2022003401

Published by
Modern History Press   www.ModernHistoryPress.com
5145 Pontiac Trail   info@ModernHistoryPress.com
Ann Arbor, MI 48105

Distributed by Ingram (USA/CAN/AU), Bertram's Books (UK/EU)
Audiobook available at Audible.com and iTunes

For Mila and Jed

Contents

If you would like to practice pronouncing the Ojibwe words in this book, we recommend the "Ojibwe People's Dictionary" online (https://ojibwe.lib.umn.edu/about-ojibwe-language)

1 ⍭ Didis (Blue Bird)

The wind gusted and blew water onto the ship's deck. Because I wore an old pair of running shoes, my feet slid across the deck's surface. I held a small book in my left hand and with my right reached out for something to hold onto to stop my sliding. I coughed and my breath seemed to freeze in the air.

I heard a persistent tapping sound. Where was it coming from? The tapping grew louder. I took a step forward until—with a jolt—I sat up and found myself wrapped tightly in my bedsheet. I had been caught in a dream. Now I was awake, and caught only in a sheet.

Tap, tap, tap, click, click, click.

I looked at the window. The tapping was coming from outside my bedroom. That pesky blue jay was back again and tapping his beak on my windowsill!

Why was he here? Was another mystery on its way? Why did his taps sound like "book, book, dig, dig?" I like books but I don't go digging in dirt to find them. What did it mean if another mystery was on its way? I didn't have time to solve another one. I had school and soccer tryouts coming up.

Last spring, I had solved the mystery behind an antique beaded necklace I'd found hidden under my closet floor. That mystery had come to me after I told my school's principal that I'd found an eagle feather on a hallway floor. Eagle feathers are sacred. Some even believe when an eagle feather drops, it means a warrior has died. The principal called one of the tribe's elders to restore the feather to a place of honor. Later, the principal told me that since I'd respected the feather, a mystery would come to me.

Maybe I shouldn't have been surprised to find the antique beaded necklace hidden under my closet floor. Our school principal sure knew what he was talking about. I then spent weeks trying to find the story behind it. I looked in old books and pored through microfilm at the library. I even talked with my grandma and other elders trying to learn the story about the necklace. After all of that, I'd learned why the mystery had come to me! I'd also learned not to get as angry about my life and I'd even made friends at my new school. Later, I had a dream. My dream told that I'd receive another mystery to solve.

Who am I? Cady Whirlwind (Wawyasto) Thunder, the Queen of Mystery?

Cady is a nickname for Cadet. My mom called me Cadet because she'd been a Girl Cadet.

"Was that like a junior version of the Girl Scouts?" I asked her.

"No, Cady, everyone thinks that. I was a crossing guard, or cadet, in elementary school. I loved being a cadet because we got to leave school early, wear a sash and walk out to stop cars and help people cross the street. Those were happy days for me, Cady, so I wanted to name you something to bring back my happy memories."

My mother left Dad and me when I was only seven. I'm not sure why. When I ask my dad he always tells me, "It's a story for another day." Then he adds, "It wasn't your fault."

Earlier tonight, before I'd turned off the little lamp on the table next to my bed, I'd thought about John Ray Chicaug. I'm waiting to turn fourteen and John Ray is almost sixteen. I have a crush on John Ray. He'd left for North Dakota earlier this summer to study with his elders. He told me before he left I wouldn't hear from him while he was gone, and he was right. He hadn't called me, or sent a text message—which didn't stop me from thinking about him every day. I know he's older than me but I still like him. When I was in the middle of investigating the necklace mystery, he helped me.

I tried to sketch him one night but gave up. Maybe someday I'll be able to draw him. He's tall, almost six feet in height. His dark brown hair is thick, cut in a blunt, straight line and almost touches his shoulders. His eyes are as dark as his hair. He's quick on his feet, probably from all the boxing he does. What I really like is that he's filled with so much energy that the air around him vibrates.

John Ray had treated me like a real person and not just a little kid. He'd seen me as a real, live girl—and he kissed me! Me, Cady! It was just a soft little peck but it was a kiss and the first one I had received from a boy.

May the Creator be with you in all which you do and say. This is my wish for John Ray.

I switched on the little lamp next to my bed, got up and walked to the window where I waved away that noisy bird. Then I retrieved the antique beaded necklace from its hiding place under my closet floor.

I held it in my hand and made my wish—to win a spot on the school's soccer team. Tomorrow was a big day, and I needed my sleep because Coach Jones was holding tryouts for the team. I'd sprained my ankle last spring and had to quit training. It wasn't a bad sprain and healed fast. I'd been running again for most of the summer.

"Even though school doesn't start for two weeks, I want the kids on my team to start practicing now. I need to get them in shape if we're going to have a successful first season." Coach had been interviewed for the rez newspaper and the paper had also placed a quarter-page ad about tryouts on the front page. The team would be coed and I wanted to be in the starting lineup.

I babysat my little brother, Colson, while Francine, my "stepmonster," worked at the donut shop. That meant I had to run early—before she left for work at 6:30 a.m. or after she got home at 3:30 p.m.

My dad didn't work a set schedule. If he was home it meant he needed quiet time to plan his classes and work on the computer and not watch Colson. My job was to keep Colson away from dad when he was working. My dad is in his fifties and teaches our native language on the reservation, which is twenty miles from Barnesville, the town where we now live in Michigan's Upper Peninsula. Francine is a lot younger. We didn't get along very well last year. This year is better, maybe it's because we've grown used to each other.

Anyway, I "digress." Digress is my new favorite word and it means to step away from something for a little bit. Last year it was "surreal," which has been overused and is worn out now because everybody uses it. "Digress" is much fancier and makes me sound older.

Tap! Tap! That pesky bird came back! Why wouldn't he leave? And why did I keep hearing the words "books, research, and ship" in my thoughts?

I walked to the window and lifted the shade a few inches. Tap, tap, tap, went his beak against the window. Morse Code or just blue jay business? I could feel my nose wrinkling up the way it does when I'm concentrating hard on something. I started to count out the seconds. I gave up when I reached twenty. Now new words repeated in my thoughts, "Irish," and "journal." Irish is my best friend. I'm telling you—she's no writer.

Journal? Was the book I held in my dreams a journal? I flopped back down on my bed. My head nestled into my favorite yellow pillow. I reached out to touch my nightstand and felt for the switch on my small lamp with the blue-and-white polka-dot lampshade. Then I changed my mind and didn't turn off the light and instead felt under my bed for my sketchbook. I grabbed it and sat back up. I opened the brass-colored clasp on its front cover and a page fell open.

I use my sketchbook for beadwork designs. I also like to draw funny cartoons of my friends. The opened page showed my latest creation—a caricature of Irish. She's got curly red hair and green eyes and pale skin covered with freckles. She likes to brag her grandparents came from County Claire in Ireland. I happen to know they own the donut shop where Francine works, and they came from Milwaukee, Wisconsin, and not Ireland. Irish's real name is Josephine.

Irish isn't native but our school has an open-door policy to all students in the area. Irish likes our school because it's in a rural, which is why she's there and how I met her.

"I like to get out of the city and enjoy nature," she once told me.

"Yeah, Irish, like Barnesville is such a bustling metropolis," her friend, Derek, joked.

"Well, it is to me," she answered back. "I just like it better out here."

Her mom started calling her Irish when she was two-years-old and threw temper tantrums lasting for almost an hour. Now everyone calls her Irish. I don't like to think about what she'd do to me if I called her Josephine or told the other kids her real name.

I'd "focused"—the word "focus" is another new favorite word and means to concentrate your interest or activity on something—on Irish's super-curly hair, intense green eyes and purple glasses (which she hardly ever wore). I put the glasses in the drawing because I knew it would make her mad. I drew her wearing one of her colorful outfits…a T-shirt with a leprechaun on its front, bright red clogs and bedazzled jeans. Irish bedazzled everything.

"I don't care if it's gone out of style. I love jewels, I love bedazzling," she told me proudly one day, stomping her foot for emphasis.

Underneath my sketch I'd written a date. I looked at the date again and was stunned. The date I'd written was tomorrow! I shook my head in disbelief—summer was almost over and school would start soon. School and tryouts for the soccer team and babysitting my baby brother. It would be easy to forget about my dream and the blue jay's visit.

Irish and her boyfriend and I planned to meet tomorrow afternoon after tryouts for the soccer team. She changed boyfriends a lot. I wondered what this one would be like. Is the mystery the blue jay wanted to tell me connected to Irish and her new boyfriend? My stomach did a somersault, which meant I was starting to worry.

Enough of this worrying. But what is the meaning behind the words the bird seemed to tap out?

I put the necklace back in its hiding place. It was too precious to me to leave out in the open. I got back into bed, turned out the light and went to sleep.

2 ⚬ Wshkeja (In the Beginning)

The next day I got up early to go running, came home, showered and gave my baby brother his breakfast. After I'd played with him for a little bit I put him in his crib for a nap. I woke him up an hour later because Dad was going to drive me out to the rez where tryouts were being held for the soccer team and he'd have to go with us.

Once we got to the soccer field, in back of the school, Coach had each of us run laps and then lined us up.

"I want each of you to show me how you'd dribble the ball down the field," he told us before blowing on his whistle.

"Listen up, guys. The first one to get the ball kicks it to Jerry and who then kicks it to Cady." He read off all of our names and added, "Once you've been passed the ball, kick it to the next person and get off the field. Got it?"

"Yes, Coach," we agreed in unison.

"I can't hear you," he bellowed at us, "That's something we'll need to work on." He blew his whistle again and we did as he'd instructed. Coach put us through more drills for the next hour and a half when he blew his whistle again.

"Huddle up. You've all made the team, but some of you are going to have to work harder to get up to speed. I'll help you with that, so will your team mates. And all of you need to earn a grade point average of at least a C. Got it? Now get out of here."

With a lot of whooping and yelling, we left the field. I even high-fived a few of the guys.

I walked over to where Dad was talking to one of the other parents and bent down to touch little Colson. He smiled up at me while sitting in his stroller waving his sippy cup.

Dad shook hands with one of his friends before looking at me.

"Congrats, Cady! Now let's go home."

An hour later we were in our kitchen, where I cleared off the counter and spread out bread, bologna, mustard and mayonnaise to make sandwiches for lunch when Francine surprised us by coming home early. It was already nearing the end of August, and my days of babysitting would soon end. School was set to start the day after Labor Day, a little more than a week away.

"Ed, I'm home. We finished up early at the donut shop. Where's my baby? Where's Colson? Who's made lunch?" she sang. The kitchen door slammed behind her. "My boss sent me home with donuts. He made too many blueberry ones, and I've got a dozen of those and a gooey caramel-frosted one for my baby."

"Why, thank you, dear," my dad said and kissed Francine's cheek. Didn't he know the caramel donut was for Colson and not for him? My baby brother would make a mess, but he'd be happy.

"How about you, Cady? Want a donut?" Dad asked.

"Dad, you know I don't like the blueberry ones. I'll make a bologna sandwich and have a dish of applesauce Grandma made for us."

"Suit yourself. We're leaving soon anyway. I promised Francine I'd take her and Colson to see her sister's family." Francine's family lived about twelve miles north of Barnesville.

"They've asked us to stay for supper," Dad continued.

"We'll be home about 8 p.m. I don't want you roaming around when we're gone. I've left a list of chores for you. When you're done, you can go to Irish's. Listen to me, I want you home by eight this evening. Understand?"

"Yes, but Dad, I need to tell you something. It's about my dream."

Dad told Francine he'd be out in a few minutes, he took me aside.

"Okay, what's this about a dream?"

After I told him that in my dream I'd been sliding around the deck of an old ship, clutching a small book in my hand, he took a deep breath.

"You want to know what it means, right? But, Cady, you must wait and see. You have been given a gift for solving mysteries. If a mystery comes to you, then you must use your gift to help solve it or you will lose the gift. You know this, we've talked about it."

"But, Dad..."

"Enough, Cady, I've got to go."

Dad and I were getting along pretty well, even Francine was easier to get along. Now that Colson was almost a one-year-old, he'd started sleeping through the night. He was eating more solid food, so he wasn't as fussy because he wasn't hungry. All this meant Dad and Francine and I were sleeping better which made us get along better because we weren't tired and crabby.

School started in two weeks, and I didn't want to get grounded. I figured I could breeze through the chores in about an hour, which would leave me almost six hours of freedom! Dad wrote a list of my chores each week in a blue spiral-bound notebook, which he kept next to the coffeepot. He wrote the list out each Sunday night, making it clear they were to be completed by Saturday noon. My list this week: wash the kitchen floor, strip the sheets from my bed and put on clean sheets, clean my bedroom and the bathroom.

"By the way, Cady, you've been pretty good about helping us out with Colson this summer. Here's twenty dollars. I know you and Irish like to hang out, I want my girl to have spending money. Don't spend it all in one place."

Dad hardly ever handed out money. He was old school and told me at least once a month, "I give you food to eat and your own bedroom. If you want anything more you'll have to earn it." When I told my older brother, Bruce, about this he just laughed. Bruce was twenty-seven-years-old and lived in Minneapolis, Minnesota.

"Yup, that's Dad. However, if you're ever in deep trouble, he'll be there for you. In the meantime, you'll have to find a job. Maybe you could babysit more? If your beadwork improved you could sell it at pow wows." Bruce couldn't help smiling when he said it. If anyone else had insulted my beadwork I'd have been mad. Bruce is the oldest of my three older brothers. He's good to me, so I let it slide. I don't know the other two because they live in California where they grew up. The four of us are half-siblings: we have the same father and different mothers.

"Thanks, Dad." I took the money and slipped it into the pocket of my jeans.

He shook his head and laughed and I could hear him mutter "women" under his breath.

"Behave yourself while we're gone. You and Irish stay out of trouble and I'll see you later tonight," he said. He tapped me on the shoulder and turned to pick up my little brother in his baby carrier.

Francine waited for him in the driveway and yelled, "Ed, come on, come on, what's keeping you? Let's get going already."

"Well, okay. We're off. *Bama pi*, Cady." The kitchen door slammed, his footsteps pounded down the back steps on his way to the car. *Bama pi* means "until we meet again." We don't have words for goodbye in our native language.

"*Bama pi*," I whispered back. I wondered if he heard me.

Two hours later my chores were done, and I ran the four blocks to meet Irish in her backyard. Waiting is something Irish doesn't do well because she's always moving, always in motion. The backyard at her mother's house looked like a kid's paradise. Irish's mom ran a daycare out of her house so the backyard had a swing set, one of those giant sandboxes shaped like a turtle with a lid to keep out stray cats, and a deck-like treehouse. Because the tree house was off limits to the little kids, you needed to drag a ladder out of its hiding place to reach it.

Irish sat on her little sister's swing and pumped her legs to their absolute limit as she swung back and forth. She jumped off when she saw me and ran up to me to give me a hug. I could hear the gum cracking in her mouth when she squeezed me. She smelled like peppermints.

"Oh, girl, I've got a surprise for you. Come on." She grabbed my hand and started running.

"Where are we going? Why are you in such a hurry?" I asked.

"Cady, you're so silly. Come on, I've got a surprise! They're waiting for us."

"Who's waiting for us? What's going on, Irish? I thought we were going to meet your new boyfriend somewhere."

"You'll see, it's a surprise. Come on, slowpoke!" She grabbed my hand and pulled me along. "Come on, we don't want to be late!"

3 ❧ Wagnogan (Wigwam)

Irish didn't slow down for almost fifteen minutes. I checked the time on my old style and beat-up silver-colored cell phone. She led me down four blocks until the Main Street intersection where she turned right and started to jog. She ran pretty fast even though she wore a pair of fur-lined pink clogs. She dropped my hand before we slowed to a complete stop. She took a deep breath and then took off again. Four blocks later we turned to the left and went another two blocks.

I'd never been in this part of town before. Most of the houses were abandoned. Some even had boards covering the windows.

"Irish, what are we doing here? What's going on?"

"You're with me, so quit worrying. It's okay." She stopped suddenly and pointed to one of the abandoned houses.

She punched me on the arm again and ran up a broken sidewalk to the house's porch.

She stopped at the porch's steps, turned and looked at me. "Come on, don't be such a scaredy-cat."

I could feel my shoulders trembling a little. Irish knew I sometimes had flashbacks to when I was a little girl. Abandoned houses were one of my triggers. I started to get mad at her for bringing me here. I shook the fear out of my shoulders and looked around.

Emptiness and loss hung in the air. Three small bicycles, each one missing parts, littered its front yard. Garbage bags lined the street in front. They'd been ripped open, probably by a stray dog. Pieces were missing from the sidewalk leading from the house's front porch to the street, and other parts were broken and jagged. Tree roots, sand and dirt pushed up through the cracks breaking the sidewalk apart. Chunks of cement had broken off from the sidewalk and were scattered through the yard. The front yard had more tall weeds growing in it than grass.

"What a mess," I said out loud as I kicked a little red plastic tractor, already missing three of its four wheels, so I didn't do much damage.

Craaassh!

What?

I looked up at the porch and saw Irish's friends, Derek and James, walking out through the house's front door and onto the porch. One of them must have found an old glass bottle on the porch's floor and kicked it. He noticed me staring at him, looked at me, and then looked down at the bottle and kicked it again. Now it lay shattered at his feet.

"Sorry, I didn't think it would make so much noise. Guess I was just excited," Derek said.

"Yeah, right," I muttered under my breath and kicked a stone out of the way.

The two boys started laughing and whooping. I wanted to stare those two boys down, when the front door opened again, and John Ray walked out to stand next to them.

"I told you I had a surprise for you. And this is a good one, right?" Irish asked me while throwing her arms around me and jumping up and down.

I whispered, "Yeah, it sure is."

My heart skipped faster and faster, and I could feel little beads of sweat start to form on my back. My eye started to twitch the way it does when I'm nervous and excited. My brain keeps telling me to calm down, but my body doesn't listen. And then I did the thing I do when I'm nervous. I held my left hand with my right and pushed the fingernail of my thumb deep into the flesh of my palm. Maybe if it hurt enough I'd know I wasn't dreaming. John Ray was here where I could see him! Why was he here? Did he know I'd be here? Did he know how I felt about him? He would always be older than me, but at least we're different clans.

Maybe one day he'd think of me as a girlfriend? If we belonged to the same clan that could never happen. Dad and Grandma had reassured me often that I was bear clan. John Ray

Chicaug was eagle clan. I knew this because our grandmas were close friends, and my grandma had told me this last spring.

"It's fitting, Cady. You're a person who likes to dig for the truth and John Ray is one who will soar high," Grandma Winnie told me that day.

But now John Ray laughed out loud, high-fived each of those goofs, Derek and James, before crossing the porch. He walked down the rickety steps and came toward me. He was wearing faded jeans and scuffed brown leather ankle boots. The design on the front of his bleached out navy T-shirt resembled a buffalo. He had pulled his hair off his face into a long braid. And his smile— what a smile! It lit up his face, it made me happy and excited and nervous all at the same time.

"I just got home last night, I've got some free time before I go back to North Dakota. I asked Irish to bring you here because I know you like mysteries. You helped solve the one about the necklace, remember?"

"I helped solve the last one? If you remember, John Ray, I solved the last one by myself." I even stamped my foot on the ground for emphasis.

Cool down, Cady, don't get so upset. It's John Ray, remember?

"Well, maybe I did have a little help," I added in a quieter voice and smiled back at him.

Squawk, squawk…The noisy talking blue jay appeared again, perched on an overhanging branch of a tree just above my head.

Even a noisy bird thinks he helped me. I muttered these words to myself and kicked at the ground.

"Yup, even your favorite blue jay knows you don't walk alone," John Ray said as he looked straight at me. Nothing ever upset him. And then he smiled his wonderful smile. His smile was a light shining on all the flowers of the earth until they burst into color.

Jaay-jaay!

That bothersome blue jay flew down and landed on the side of the porch as if inviting us to sit down and make ourselves comfortable, so the five of us perched on the steps. Irish sat between Derek and James on the top step, John Ray sat one step down from them. I claimed the bottom step and stretched my legs out in front of me.

"Okay, guys, listen up," John Ray said after snapping his fingers to get our attention. "This house wasn't always this beat up. My grandpa said his half-brother had lived here. Back then it was one of the nicest houses in town. When grandpa's brother died he left the house to my aunt. She lived here until ten years ago when she had a stroke and was moved out of state.

"After that, the house was rented out for a while, but Grandpa said no one in the family knew the renters had moved on. My aunt was too sick to take care of things. It was a big misunderstanding! Everybody thought someone else was taking care of the house," John Ray told us.

"My aunt died a few weeks ago and left the house to my grandpa. He's been laid up since her death. He had a hip replacement and is still recovering, so he asked me to check on the house. He wants me to dig for something buried in the backyard. I'll need some volunteers to help me."

And then he looked at Irish and me.

John Ray spoke in a matter-of-fact way. He sounded like a grownup and not like the boys in my classes at school. I felt a little ashamed for what I'd said about the house once I learned it belonged to his grandpa.

"I'm sorry I said this house was a wreck, John Ray. I didn't know your grandpa owned it."

The patch of trees surrounding the house was sparse enough for the sun to filter through the leaves, giving the house a scary look. My shoulders shivered a little. I trusted John Ray more than anyone and wondered what the mystery was surrounding this abandoned place. Some windows were missing and others were broken. There could be squirrels and spiders and mice and maybe even bats inside.

"Okay, guys, let the adventure begin! Grandpa drew a map for me so we'd know where to dig. Who wants to help me turn over some dirt and find what we're looking for? It must be important for my grandpa to have sent me here the day after I got back from North Dakota. According to this map he drew, we've got to start by going back into the house and walking out its back door."

John Ray stood up, turned, and walked across the porch. He looked over his shoulder and said, "Come on." He propped the front door open with an old brick and walked inside. Derek, James, Irish, and I followed him inside.

The house was empty and dark.

A long time ago someone in John Ray's family once made their home here, though it sure isn't much today.

Irish keeps telling me I'm too judgmental (one of my favorite words from sixth grade, and means being overly critical), so I tried to empty my head to see the house with clear eyes for what it had once been and not for what existed now.

The five of us walked into the main room, which was about the size of a small classroom. It had tipped-over broken chairs, a busted-up Barbie doll missing both its legs, and a brown-and-green toy metal truck resting on its bent axle.

"Looks like some little kids used to live here," Derek said.

"What was your clue, genius?" Irish asked him. Then she gave him one of her big hugs and he was smiling so much I know he didn't notice the insult.

I spun around and then walked over to the room's one big window. I had a feeling of déjà vu. Déjà vu is French and another one of my favorite things to say. It means feeling as if you've already been somewhere and you're now there again. Had I been here before?

John Ray stood in front of the window, looking out toward the street. The sun shone through the window's rippled old glass, making a rainbow around him. My head buzzed, and I felt as if I was spinning around and around. What was happening? Sometimes, I just feel overwhelmed.

4 ⚡ Wanket (Dig)

My head stopped spinning as quickly as it had started. Maybe this nervous energy was because I was near John Ray?

Derek and James started telling knock-knock jokes. I guess no one told them those jokes are for little kids, even though the jokes were silly and stupid and kind of funny. Anyway, they're Irish's friends and not mine. They're both Ojibway. John Ray and I are Potawatomi. Most people don't understand that just because we're Indian we're not all alike. Different tribes have different customs, traditions, and languages.

There must have been something in the air because they were laughing and pushing each other.

"Hey Cady, look at me!" Irish shouted and then she danced one of her little jig dances.

"Yeah, great, Irish," I muttered under my breath.

"Really, guys?" John Ray asked them. "I want to talk to Cady about something so you three can move to another room," he told them. His quiet tone told us he was serious.

"No way. Where Cady goes, I go," Irish answered back.

And then Derek interrupted, "And where Irish goes, we go. Right, James?

"Uh, most of the time. This place gives me the creeps. I've got to go. I've got things to do and it's important stuff," James answered back.

"Real important. Like, you better cut your dad's lawn before he gets home from work," Irish sang out. "James is going to cut the lawn, so he doesn't end up his dad's pawn," she added for good measure and then danced a little jig again.

"Cut it out, Irish, or you're not going for a ride in my older brother's new Mustang," James snapped back.

"Oh, yeah, I forgot. Sorry, see you two later. I'm sticking around here with Cady and John Ray. Text me later, OK?"

Irish didn't seem too upset when James and Derek turned to leave, because she immediately grabbed my hand and then John Ray's.

John Ray looked at Irish and then at me.

"Follow me," he instructed. He walked out of the room and into a dark hallway leading to a back door. He pulled a screwdriver with an amber-colored plastic handle from his back pocket and inserted it into the rusted lock on the door. The door stuck when he first tried to open it. He moved the screwdriver back and forth several times until the lock opened. The door made a creaking sound when he pulled it open.

John Ray turned his head to look at me and smiled. Then he crooked his finger, indicating we should follow him out to the back porch. He stood there less than a minute before he disappeared!

A minute or two later I heard his wonderful laughter booming up to where Irish and I stood.

"Hey, Cady, don't look so worried. There aren't any steps back here, so I jumped off the deck into this huge pile of dried leaves. You two can do it; it's not much of a jump," he shouted.

Irish took a step back before she pushed me off the back deck. I fell through the air and landed into a pile of leaves on the ground where there should have been back steps. The wind had heaped the leaves about a foot or two in height. They were crisp and dry and showed different shades of red and brown. They softened my landing. I loved the swishing noise they made and when I moved my arms their scent filled the air. For a few moments I smelled the woods, a musty mixture of moss and earth. It smelled of nature and not of manufactured perfumes. I closed my eyes for a minute and drew the woodsy scent into me until someone grabbed my arm and started shaking me.

Irish smiled in her goofy way and stared into my face. "Hey, silly, see. No big deal, right?" She used a sing-song sort of tone when she didn't want anyone to know she was nervous and she sang those words in a quivering voice.

Irish looked at John Ray. "Hey, we're here now. Where are we going to go?"

He stood about four yards from us, turned, and pointed southward to an abandoned garage about one hundred feet away. The garage looked as deserted and beat up as the house.

"Down there," he told us.

"No way," Irish said, "wasn't that Old Joe's garage? It gives me the creeps."

Because Irish had lived her entire life in Barnesville, and John Ray had lived on the reservation nearby, they knew about places I didn't. I'd just moved here last year from Minnesota.

John Ray took off at a trot. I followed pulling Irish along with me. Like the house, the garage's windows were either broken or missing. Spider webs hung everywhere. I remembered reading that in the past the old ones gathered spider webs to use as bandages. They would clump the webs together and put them on the wound. The squat wooden building had a forlorn look. Its gray paint was faded and weathered, and a field of weeds had sprung up around it. Part of the roof had started to sag. I felt a shudder start again in my shoulders.

The garage itself looked big enough to hold three pickup trucks and a bunch of tools.

"John Ray, this is creepy," Irish whispered. "I'm not going any closer and neither is Cady. I'm going home. You're coming with me. Right, Cady?"

"I don't know," I muttered.

"Don't worry about her, Irish, I'll make sure she gets home safely," John Ray told her.

Irish shot me a look. She looked puzzled and hurt, then flashed a smile.

"John Ray, I wish your grandpa was here to help you dig, I get it that he's laid up. Call me, Cady, OK? I'm out of here."

Irish always talked big and told us she wasn't afraid of anything. She called me a scaredy-cat. Now she was the one who left.

5 ⋄ *Mozhwet* (Cut Hair)

John Ray cleared some fallen branches and dead leaves from an old stone bench nearby and motioned me to sit next to him. I tapped my right foot up and down on the ground. I could feel the sweat forming in my hands. I was happy to be with John Ray. I was happy he needed my help but I was also nervous. What were we doing here ?

"Why did those other guys take off running when they knew you wanted to come here?" I asked him.

"It's because of the superstition about this garage. My grandpa told me Old Joe owned this garage for most of his life, through good times and bad, from the 1950s to the early 1990s. Joe was part Indian, Grandpa told me. He stood about five feet seven inches tall and wore his long hair gathered into a ponytail at the back of his neck. He tucked it inside the collar of his overalls, always the same pair of greasy-looking gray ones. He had a tattoo of a shield with a wolf in its center on his left forearm. He called it his medicine.

"My grandpa told me Old Joe would joke with his customers saying, 'My medicine is strong, it's why I fix cars so good.' Grandpa said when Old Joe smiled he didn't seem to care about showing the world a few of his teeth were missing. 'I can still eat good so what does it matter. Those dentist guys scare me,' my grandpa would say quoting Old Joe."

John Ray then told me his grandpa had told him it was a joke around the reservation community that Rose, Old Joe's wife, had accidentally thrown out her husband's dentures. One Christmas season she had been so busy cleaning up after a party, she hadn't noticed her husband's false teeth had fallen into a pile of wrapping paper after someone had knocked them off a table. Old Joe had taken them out and set them down after a long day of entertaining guests while looking for relief from his poorly fitting "choppers."

Even though this story was sort of interesting, I still wondered why John Ray had brought me here.

"Why are we here, John Ray? What's going on?"

"Hang on, Cady, I'll get to it. I promise you this mystery is a good one. I grew up hearing my dad and his friends talking about Old Joe. Mostly it was about his skill at fixing engines and carburetors. They said he could work magic with his fingers and could get any old wreck running and keep it running. 'He's so good with the old beaters,' my dad would say laughing, "just think what he could do with a good car."

We both laughed out loud a little, then John Ray said, "Ok, Cady. Back to my story. The day after Rose accidentally threw out Old Joe's false teeth, Old Joe had to rush her to the hospital. Later we found out she'd been sick and didn't want anyone to know until complications set in, so she couldn't hide it any longer. We learned later she'd also had a heart condition since childhood. She died two days later. Old Joe never replaced his dentures."

"Hmm, it's a sad story. Even sort of romantic isn't it, John Ray?"

"It's weird you think it's romantic, so I'm going to get back to my story. Old Joe cut his hair as a sign of mourning Rose because it's one of our customs. Cutting our hair short shows our sadness at losing someone we love.

"After Rose's death, Joe changed. For a while he stopped working on cars and didn't clean the garage or the yard around it. Some people even said he'd started drinking because he'd started to slur his words some of the time or even stumble now and then. Years later we know he wasn't drinking but that he had a disease. His black hair even turned white the night she died, he was still kind of young, at least too young for white hair. When I asked how folks knew that, my grandpa said they could when his hair grew back and they saw that it was white. After the four days of the sacred fire for Rose, people forgot about him."

I remembered what my Dad had taught me about holding a sacred fire after someone dies. The fire is kept burning for four days and four nights to aid the spirit as it crosses over.

"My grandpa said Old Joe never forgot about Rose. He still had some customers at the garage and everyone just assumed he was okay. He must have been very sad to let his house fall apart the way it did," John Ray added.

He looked down at the dirt and then stood up and started walking and kicking away pieces of broken cement and loose stones. He kept kicking stones and gravel until he reached a corner of the garage where he knelt down and pushed dead leaves into a pile.

"Aha, this will do!" he said. He found an old spade nearby and waved it back and forth over the pile.

"Here, I brought this for you." He pulled a small garden trowel from his jacket pocket and handed it to me. "Time to start digging."

"Digging? Are you nuts? It's going to get dark soon, besides I don't know what we're digging for."

"Bones, Cady, bones."

6 ⚡ Mkek (Box)

"Uh huh, John Ray, no way, I don't dig for bones. Not ever," I told him.

John Ray had already started digging. Even though the sun still shone, it felt as if we were in shade. The air surrounding the little patch of dirt we were working in felt heavy. I looked up to see a few clouds start to fill the sky above us, and turned to walk away.

Even though I didn't know my way around this side of town, I told myself running home alone sure beat digging up bones in a deserted and creepy backyard. Because my dad was raised as a traditional Indian, he'd taught me the importance of bones. Bones are sacred. Indian people value the remains of our ancestors and consider our burial sites to be holy places because our ancestors' bones are buried there. Were we being disrespectful? Would we anger the spirits of the ancestors who might be buried here by tampering with a gravesite? I knew John Ray knew better. And was there really a gravesite in the backyard of a deserted house in town? Something didn't make sense.

I took the garden tool from John Ray's outstretched hand and started to rub the handle of it back and forth with the palm of my right hand. With my left hand I swatted away a lazy fly, then I couldn't help it. I spat. I wanted to spit out the bad taste in my mouth for what we were about to do, I tried not to cry.

I looked up at John Ray. I wondered if he could tell that I was nervous and fidgety. He had such a kind face that I started to calm down. When it came down to it, I trusted John Ray. He was that kind of boy.

"Relax, Cady. We're not digging for human bones or any other kind of bones. I was just teasing you." As he said these words, I remembered that he honored and respected his grandfather who had helped raise him in the traditional way. And then I wondered if he was testing me. Would I be willing to do anything he asked? I shook my head to get rid of that thought.

"Then what are we looking for?" My words sounded squeaky even though I tried to sound brave and confident.

"A box Old Joe buried out here somewhere. We need to find it."

"Why?" I asked.

"Because Old Joe told me to."

"You're having visions now?"

"No, it's because my grandpa asked me to. Just help me dig, okay. Please?"

Right from the start I had a feeling John Ray hadn't brought us out to Old Joe's garage to dig because he thought it would be an adventure. I couldn't prove it, so I wasn't going to question him. He told me he was doing it for his grandpa. I'd do what he asked because I liked him, and I wanted him to like me. Ever since I'd met him, I'd had a crush on him, but I never thought that being with him would mean we'd be digging in his relative's backyard.

I followed him from the front of the garage and down to a patch of yard at its back. I knelt down a few feet from where John Ray had started to dig. I pushed the trowel into the dirt. I pushed and wiggled and rooted around with it for about twenty minutes until I felt blisters start to form on my hand. I tried to act like a tough kid, even though I wanted to cry. I don't like blisters, they hurt. I also like to draw in my sketchbook every night, and I knew the blisters would make my fingers clumsy. My sketches wouldn't turn out the way I wanted them to, and that would make me mad.

And then I remembered talks I'd had with my older half-sister, Grace, when she visited us for a month each summer. We have different mothers but we shared the same dad. When she visited we'd set up a cot in my bedroom and we'd talk late into the night, or one of us fell asleep.

I remembered one of her favorite sayings, "A faint heart never wins." Back then I wasn't sure what she meant because, Grace liked to recite this phrase whenever I asked her about something. It was her standard answer for every question I threw at her. Did she mean I had to keep digging when my hands hurt just because I wanted someone to like me?

"John Ray, I need to take a break. My hand hurts," I shouted to him because he had moved further away from me and had started digging in a new spot.

And once again that same blue jay was following me and making those squeaky, clicking sounds.

"*Ahau*, I've found something!" he yelled and stood up. He waved it in the air and then brushed the dirt off by rubbing it against his leg. (*Ahau* is another one of my favorite words. In our way it means *Come on, okay*.)

"Sorry, false alarm, guess we need to keep digging." He showed me an old black boot missing half its sole. He tossed it aside but a few minutes later I heard his excited shout once again.

"This is it, I know it is this time!" he shouted.

I looked at him and saw him waving a beat-up brown package in the air.

"What'd you find, John Ray?" I asked. I was tired and cranky. My hand hurt from the blisters forming and my shoulders were slumped. I brushed a tear from my eye. "I'd like to know. I worked hard and my hands hurt. Don't I get to know what you found?"

"I agree. Here's the reason we were digging." His outstretched hands held a small birchbark box about the size of a pencil box.

"This box was wrapped in a piece of water-resistant oilcloth. Grandpa described it pretty well. I know this is it. He told me not to open it before I show it to him. I'll meet with him and then I'll tell you what I learn at the coffee shop tomorrow. Meet me there about four, okay?"

I watched as he slipped the small package into his backpack.

And then that annoying blue jay came back and started squawking at me and fluttering its wings. It was time to leave. I wanted to stay and ask John Ray more, but I didn't want to get in trouble with my dad. If I broke my curfew, then I couldn't meet John Ray tomorrow.

Could the blue jay read my thoughts? I wanted to yell at the bird, "Now what? What is it this time?"

That bird answered me by flying down from a branch a few feet above and landing on my left arm. I heard his blue jay noises with my ears while at the same time, inside my head, I heard him say, *"See here, Cady. Plenty of people love you. You can't see them, they're here and they're blessing you. Now go and do as your friend tells you. Cady, haven't you forgotten something?"*

"Oh, my gosh," I laughed in embarrassment and stopped walking. I had forgotten to put tobacco down. When we take plants from the earth, we never take all of what we are searching for but leave some of it behind. I wasn't sure what John Ray had taken other than the small brown package. Even so, I wanted to honor the earth where we'd been digging and leave an offering. I withdrew a small leather pouch from my hoodie pocket, loosened its leather thong tie, emptied some of the *sema* (tobacco) into my

left hand. I shook it into my right hand and bent down and placed a bit of the *sema* on the ground.

When I stood John Ray said, "Good job, Cady. *Megwetch.*"

Megwetch means thank you in our language. I told him it was getting late. I didn't want to make my dad mad, so I had to leave. He patted his backpack, straightened up and said, "I'll race you home, okay?"

I ran home with John Ray running a few feet behind me. I thought of something Grandma had told me when I heard him singing as he followed me.

"Some people can sing the clouds out of the sky," she'd said, then laughed.

John Ray was one of those kinds of singers.

7 ≉ Yajmowen (Story)

I made it home before my dad's curfew.

"Glad to see you home, Cady. We're calling it an early night and turning in soon," he told me.

"This baby is driving me nuts. It's off to bath time for you, little guy. Are you coming up soon, Ed?" Francine asked my dad.

"I'll be up soon; I just need to finish a few things down here first. Give the baby his bath and I'll see you soon," Dad answered. Then he looked at me and winked.

"Who are you and what have you done with my dad?" I asked him.

"Whoa, Cady, lighten up. I had a good day for a change." He stood and walked into the kitchen. "Where's the crockpot?" he hollered out.

"In the cupboard above the refrigerator where only you can reach it," I answered back. I remembered to smile. We're finally getting along again, and I didn't want to make him mad and end up grounded or punished or sent to my room until the end of time.

Dad is a pretty good cook. He learned in the Army. It's a good thing because Francine can't cook at all other than making hot dogs and Twinkie cakes and bringing home donuts. I'm just learning how to cook.

Dad took the box of oatmeal from the cupboard and poured it into a measuring cup. "Watch me, Cady, and pay attention. I'm mixing one cup of steel cut oats with one cup of chopped dry fruit and four cups of water. I'm adding one teaspoon each of pumpkin pie spice and cinnamon and two tablespoons of brown sugar and a bit of maple syrup for flavoring. I'll put it in the crockpot on low overnight. Eight hours is good. With this cooker, I can program it to switch to warm after that. We'll have it ready in the morning and serve it with milk. It should be good."

It would smell warm and spicy as it cooked, a reassuring smell telling me everything was fine, making me feel safe and loved. I liked those feelings.

He hummed an old-timey country song as he stirred the oatmeal. I decided to chance it and touched his shoulder.

"Uh, dad, have you ever heard of Old Joe?"

"Why are you asking, Cady? All of it happened so long ago."

"I saw some of the kids today and they were talking about him and telling stories and stuff. I don't know what to believe sometimes," I told him.

"Every few years those stories start going around. Your Grandma told me about him. I remember some of the townspeople saying they'd seen Old Joe walking through the fields to his garage, or in his overalls at the muffler shop in town trying to help the guys there put in a new muffler on the tribal chairman's car. This scared a few folks because they said all of it happened after he died. Some of the women from the elders group said they'd spotted Old Joe, or his spirit, at Rose's grave in the reservation cemetery. One old lady said she'd even seen him putting food into the little spirit house on top of Rose's grave."

I knew about spirit houses from my grandma's teachings. She'd taken me with her to put food at a relative's spirit houses in a private family cemetery. A spirit house is a small wooden house placed on top of the grave. People place food in it for the spirit of the deceased, so he or she has the strength needed to move on to the next world. In later years, food is left at the spirit houses to feed their spirit. In earlier times the houses were made out of birchbark or rush mats. These days they're built of wood.

Dad wiped his hands on a paper towel and turned to go up the back staircase to the bedroom he shared with Francine and the baby. He gave me a final look before starting up the stairs.

"And, Cady, be sure to check the front door is locked before you come upstairs, okay?"

"Sure, Dad," I answered, knowing he'd already locked up. He was super nervous about break-ins, especially since my baby brother's birth.

I poured myself a glass of apple juice and plunked down on our old gold-colored velvet couch. The worn-down fabric of the cushions made a satisfying "pouf" sound as I landed on it. I got out my sketchbook and tried to write down everything I remembered from earlier today. My hands still hurt from their blisters. I held a pencil as best I could, awkwardly, and managed to scribble a few words and a rough sketch.

After I got to the part about the blue jay, I remembered what John Ray's story about his family and Old Joe. Old Joe was a brother to John Ray's grandpa which made him John Ray's great-uncle. This could be a part of the mystery, but how did these puzzle pieces fit together?

John Ray had asked me to meet him the next day at Java Beans, the little coffee shop across the street from the public library. Dad wasn't home but I asked Francine if it was okay.

"Sure, just be home in time for dinner," she told me. "I'll clear it with your dad once he gets home."

"But, Cady, this is not a date and you've got one hour, that's it. Fifteen minutes to get there, thirty minutes to talk and another fifteen to run home. I'll call Betty, the owner of the coffee shop, and tell her to keep an eye out for you. Your dad should be home in a few minutes and he'll be watching the clock.

"Oh, and Cady. Your dad talked to me about John Ray. He said he's a fine young man who is starting to become aware of his traditional responsibilities. So, don't get too attached to him until you're older. Got it?"

"Yes, Francine, I've got it."

I never knew if Dad was joking when he'd told me, "When you're seventeen or eighteen we'll see about boy stuff."

Sometimes, I couldn't wait until I turned eighteen but meeting up with John Ray wasn't really a date. I was meeting him to find out more about the box we'd dug up.

I practically flew out the door and ran the ten blocks to the coffee shop. The sun shone and the temperature rested in the high sixties. I felt a trickle of sweat starting to form across the back of my neck, and slowed down two blocks before I arrived at the coffee shop. I didn't want to be sweaty for my meeting with John Ray.

Java Beans was a small shop tucked between a tattoo parlor and a bike shop. I didn't like coffee, but would rather have the ginger ale they served there. The mugs were always frosty, and they served all their cold drinks with fresh ice chips.

Looking through the window, I saw John Ray sitting at a booth in the back cradling a mug of coffee in his hands. A little bell hung over the shop's front door. It made a cling-clang-cling chime as I entered the shop. Then its talking bird clock announced the hour. Four o'clock was woodpecker time. I jumped a little at the tap, tap, tap noise it made.

Cinnamon and vanilla smells filled the air. Chocolate chip cookies were baking and my stomach grumbled a little with

hunger. The shop's few customers were working on their laptops.

John Ray is polite and thoughtful, not like those goofs Derek and James. He even stood up and held out a chair for me, just like the last time we'd met here, which made me happy and nervous at the same time. I can manage a chair on my own but I wondered if this is what older kids did on real dates. Maybe Irish would know? "Ney," I could hear her laughing at me if I asked her.

"Do you want a ginger ale? I'm buying," he said and waved his wallet in the air.

"Sure, sounds good."

"One ginger ale coming up. I remember you like the kind they make here in town, right?"

I nodded and watched him as he walked to the counter to order the soda. He always looked so good. His black jeans matched the black Western-style shirt he wore. The shirt's pearl buttons reflected the light and seemed to shimmer in the shop's muted lighting. And then I noticed the new silver cuff he wore on his left wrist.

John-Ray drank his coffee with a little cream and lots of sugar instead of one of those fancy coffee drinks with whipped cream and caramel and stuff. My Dad and my older brother, Bruce, drank their coffee the same way John Ray did.

He came back to the table carrying a bottle of ginger ale in his right hand and a frosted mug in his left. He set both down on the table, and I reached for the bottle to pour it into the mug. The golden-colored ginger ale bubbled and fizzed as it hit the crushed ice. I ripped the paper covering off the straw. As I took a first sip I started to relax.

I'd almost finished drinking the ginger ale before I noticed the package he'd taken from his pocket and put on the table in front of us.

"Open it," he told me.

I hesitated, "Are you sure? It looks old, and I don't want to break it."

"It's okay, Cady. That's only an old piece of cracked oilcloth wrapped around it. The wrapping isn't important; what matters is what's inside."

I carefully unwrapped the package.

"Do you know what it is?"

"I think so. Isn't it a birchbark box with quillwork?" I'd never held a piece of quillwork before and had only seen pictures of it.

"It is. It's very old, so be careful."

I held the box in my hand and then set it on the table. In my head I was picturing how I would sketch it.

"It's okay, Cady. You can open the box."

I glanced back at John Ray and then very carefully lifted the box's top. Inside was an even smaller packet also wrapped in aged oilcloth. I unwrapped it and found a journal! It was a little longer than the length of my pointer finger and maybe three inches wide. Someone had carved the name Abe into the faded brown leather cover.

"You can open it, Cady," John Ray told me. "Abe left a few notes in it. The book contains another mystery for you to solve. That's what Abe's notes are about. I have to head back to North Dakota tomorrow, so I'm leaving it with you. When I come back, you can fill me in on what you find. You like puzzles, don't you?"

"Well, sometimes, but this one might be too much for me. And why does the cover have the name Abe on it?"

"Because Abe is the name of the person who wrote in that little journal. Read the first page and you'll see why."

Carefully, very carefully, I opened the little book. Although the handwriting was small, each letter was beautifully formed. I liked its opening message.

My name is Abe and this journal is a log of my trips sailing on the Great Lakes. It's easy to forget dates and trips so I'm recording my journeys. Someday I hope to share this with my twin brother. I think we're a lot alike.

"John Ray, this is like reading history." My mind raced, thinking of how excited, and maybe even frightened, Abe must have been as he wrote this page.

"It sounds like his job was scary. I've seen how big the waves can get out on the lake. Maybe he thought he wouldn't come back one day?

"I think my grandpa might agree with that. Anyway, he said this box and the journal are a piece of our family history. For some reason he wants you to read it and then talk to him about it."

"But, why? I'm just a kid. I don't understand," I told John Ray. "This is a lot to handle. First, you have me help you dig, and now you give me the birchbark box and ask me to read the journal hidden inside of it. And, finally, your grandpa wants to talk to me about it." My stomach fluttered. I placed my hand over it to calm myself down.

"Grandpa has his ways. He can be mysterious at times. You could ask Irish to help you figure this one out—it might keep her out of trouble."

"Ney," I laughed. Irish could be pretty clever when she wanted to be but maybe she could actually help me.

Just then the coffee shop's clock made loud bird noises announcing the hour.

"I've got to get home, John Ray, or I'll be in trouble." I stood up and pushed my chair back. I looked at him again and added, "All of us will miss you." Deep inside I knew I was telling him I'd miss him.

I picked up the package and slipped it into the pocket of my jean jacket. I turned around so John Ray wouldn't see me wipe a solitary tear from my eye.

"I'll miss you, too, Cady. Want to race to the old grocery store near your house?"

I checked the clock on the wall as we left. I still had fifteen minutes to make it home. I refused to let John Ray give me a head start. I beat him to my house. He smiled when he caught up to me and kept on running.

Something had changed in John Ray. He seemed older, and even though he liked to tease me, he always treated me with respect.

Bama pi, I whispered.

I shrugged my shoulders and watched as he ran off. Once again, I wished I was older.

Another mystery was given to me to solve. And why did John Ray think I could solve it by the time he returned home? If he knew when that would be, why hadn't he told me? John Ray was like my dad and grandma, they believed that things happened in their own time. I was a procrastinator, I liked to put things off.

Another dilemma and not a good one. Do I hurry to solve this mystery or do I let the answer come to me?

After dinner, I took a bag of garbage out to the trash can next to our garage. It was dark enough to see the stars. I wondered what it would be like to be up there and looking down at earth. Did the stars know things I didn't know?

8 ⸱ Gawye (Quill)

"What have you got there, Cady?" Dad asked me the day after I'd met John Ray at the coffee shop.

I nestled deeper into an old green beanbag chair in our living room. The baby smiled and cooed as he jumped in his bouncy walker. Francine had gone out on errands, and Dad was in the kitchen cutting up vegetables. I could hear the noise the knife made as he chopped. He did it so fast and with such skill. I'd probably cut my fingers up if I tried to copy him.

"It's just practice, Cady. Practice makes perfect, something I learned in the military," he'd tell me. This is another one of my older sister's favorite sayings and now I know where it came from.

"It's something John Ray gave me yesterday," I told him.

"Hmm, birchbark and it looks old. Let me have a closer look."

I handed him the box and watched him as he turned it over and over in his hands. I think he was so absorbed in looking at the box that he let slide that I'd met John Ray. Thankfully, he didn't ask me about him but about the box.

"Your grandpa collected birchbark. Have I ever told you this about him?"

"No," I was surprised because Dad hardly ever talked about his father.

"He used to go out to collect birchbark in the spring.'"

I must have looked confused because Dad sat down next to me.

"That's when the leaves of the birch trees unfold completely and when the sap is flowing. That's when the birchbark can be peeled easily from the tree."

"Didn't it hurt the tree?"

"Not if done in the right way, we honor it by using it. The bark will get tough and grow back for the winter. Grandpa was very careful, and he knew the best time of year to do it and how not harm the tree. He took his time and made sure the used pieces made from only the outer bark of the tree. Remember, he knew the best time of year to do this. Birchbark is quite remarkable. It can't be hurt by the sun or water. Folks used it to make huts, dishes, and canoes. The smaller trees have thinner bark.

"The piece you're holding has been added to with quillwork. Quillwork has always been an interest of mine. Grandpa showed me how to do it when I was a young boy. I used to visit him during the summer months. He knew the importance of passing down our traditions and crafts. Quills are used predominantly on bark," he added.

"The quills come from porcupines. Right?"

"You're correct, Cady. The quills are usually white with a brown tip. They get their colors from natural dyes. For example, you get a yellow color from cane flower petals boiled with pieces of decayed oak bark or with the roots of cattail. You can get red from choke cherry buffalo berry or wild plum. Wild grapes give a black color to the quills and evergreen will give you..."

"Don't tell me. Green?"

"Yes, and what about your favorite color—purple?"

Dad threw me off with his question. I looked around the room and saw a bowl left on the table from somebody's snack. Inside the bowl were the dregs of cereal and what looked like dried-up fruit.

"Blueberries?" I asked and tried to make my voice sound sure of itself.

"Yes, blueberries and blackberries can be boiled down to make a dye for the quills," Dad answered. I remember my uncle telling me you could also boil walnut shells for a nice brown color.

"Our people used them a lot for decoration in the days before we started using glass beads. We decorated our clothing and birchbark utensils back before the Europeans came here. Many years later, during the nineteenth and twentieth centuries, people sold their quillwork for money, which was important to many families."

He crossed the room and started rummaging around in the bookcase.

"Here's one of Grandpa's old books. You should be able to find out more about quillwork in there. Your box looks old and the colors have faded a lot. It must have been something back in the day."

The quillwork and birchbark were interesting. I wondered if the little box held a clue to the journal? If it did, what was the clue?

"Dad, even though it's old, I think it's still something. It's also a clue of some kind for me to figure out."

"That could be," he replied before going upstairs.

I stayed in the living room absorbed in my grandpa's old book, until 9:30 p.m. when Dad called down to me.

"Tomorrow's another day. Get up here and get to bed, Cady."

I started to protest, but secretly, I was glad to be sent to my room. I had a nice supply of flashlights hidden in the drawer of the little cupboard next to my bed.

"Sure, see you tomorrow," and I grabbed the quillwork box with its little journal and started to stomp up to my room. A minute or two later I thought about my sleeping baby brother. I didn't want to wake him up, so I stopped stomping and tiptoed to my bedroom.

I rummaged through the drawer of the cupboard next to my bed looking for my favorite flashlight. Sometimes things seem to happen like magic, or it's serendipity. (Another of my new favorite words. It means when things start to happen in a really happy way.) After I'd found the flashlight and switched it on, my hand touched one of my dad's old books about native craft work. I'd probably stuck it in the drawer last year when I was struggling with a bead project for school. I flipped open the pages and discovered a chapter about quillwork!

The description started out by stating that you need to soften the quills by wetting them before fastening to birchbark or a leather hide to form patterns. When you're done, it looks like embroidery.

I was proud of my ancestors for figuring out something this important and amazing. I'd seen items decorated with seeds, shells and animal teeth at my relatives' homes, at school, and at pow wows. I'd even seen quillwork before, but I never saw it the way you do when you focus on seeing something. And now I was studying it! Tomorrow I'd use the camera in my old flip phone to take a photo of the pattern. I'd also make a sketch of it and try to find out if the design on the box had some sort of special meaning.

Too excited to sleep, I opened the lid of the box and removed the old journal. I unwrapped it carefully from the oilcloth covering. The journal's cover was cracked and stained and the sinew used in the whip stitching around its outside edges had turned darker with age. Although the pages were faded, the writing on them remained readable.

I started to lift back the cover when I heard someone pounding on my bedroom door.

"Cady, put out the light and get to sleep. It's after ten, and I've had it. See you in the morning. I'm waiting here until that light goes out."

I turned off the flashlight. I planned to wait until I heard my dad's bedroom door shut and then turn my flashlight back on. But I couldn't help it, and started to fall asleep.

* * *

Dad and Francine sometimes let me sleep later on the weekends. Lately they'd been telling me I needed to help out more in the kitchen. Francine didn't like cooking and Dad was teaching me to cook.

I like to stay up late and then sleep late the next morning, which didn't work too well on school nights or on days when I needed to get up early to watch Colson.

Today was Saturday and my day to make breakfast. I got up about 7:30 a.m., put on my gray pants and a vintage Beatles T-shirt of my older brother, Bruce's, and went downstairs to the kitchen. I made a pot of coffee and added some cinnamon to it the way my dad liked, and took a can of frozen orange juice from the freezer. I mashed it up in a pitcher I'd filled with cold water and got out bread for toast and jam. Because Colson ate finger foods now, I didn't need to fill bottles with baby formula. Instead I got out his sippy cup. I smiled when I thought of how he liked to bang his little cup on the tray of his high chair.

I looked up at the kitchen wall clock. It was in the shape of a cat. Its eyes rolled, the tail swung back and forth, and the thing drove me nuts! My dad and Francine thought it was cute. They'd won it at bingo last year. I put a pot on the stove to make oatmeal. I'd probably burn the oatmeal because I'm just learning how to make it. If it burned, I planned to cover the burn taste with dried cranberries and brown sugar the way my grandma taught me.

Even though my hands still had a few blisters from digging at Old Joe's with John Ray, it was worth it. I faced a new mystery to solve, which would help the days go faster until he came back to ask me what I had found out about the birchbark box and journal. I didn't want to disappoint John Ray and his family, but I wasn't sure how to start solving this mystery.

I told myself to be careful around a hot stove and hot pans. I didn't need more blisters or burns. I didn't like my hands. My fingers weren't long and elegant. They were short and stubby and I chewed my nails when I was nervous. My hands were good for changing my baby brother's diapers, making breakfast, and digging holes in the ground. I couldn't even grow my nails long enough to wear nail polish, and now I had blisters on my palms. I thought of the beautiful quillwork on the birchbark box we'd found. Would I ever be able to make something as wonderful and lovely with these hands?

Don't go there, Cady. Think of something positive, think of the journal and what's inside it.

I wanted to go upstairs and read whatever secrets the old journal held. Could it be related to Old Joe? I set my glass of juice down on the counter. Dad came into the kitchen holding Colson, and plopped the baby in his highchair. Dad started to pour himself a cup of coffee when we heard someone pounding on the back door.

"Cady, come on, I need you!"

"What the...?" Dad walked to the door and yanked it open.

Irish stood there. Her hair hung in a droopy mess, and she wore an old pair of red plaid flannel pajama bottoms and a faded sweatshirt. Irish's style is a bit crazy and colorful, but her hair is always perfect. She spends hours making her hair look like she doesn't fuss with it. She's what you'd call well-put together, but this morning, she looked a hot mess. Her cheeks were flushed as red as her hair, and I could see beads of sweat on her face.

"Cady, come with me. Hi, Cady's dad. Can she come with me? I need to talk to her!"

"Uh, sure. Be back in an hour, Cady." Caught by surprise, my dad agreed.

Irish grabbed my hand and pulled me out the door.

"What's so important? Geez, I didn't even eat yet."

"You've got to see this! Please, please, come with me."

"Like I've got a choice," I said as she pulled me along. We covered the three blocks to her house in a blur.

"Look, do you see it?" She pointed to an open area next to an old toolshed in the backyard of her house. A blue jay rested on top of a stack of wood near where Irish pointed. He dipped his head and then pointed his beak in the direction of the shed. And then he did it again.

I looked at Irish, she looked at me, and then we both looked at the bird. He dipped his head and then pointed his beak and did it over and over and over.

"I think he wants us to go in the shed," Irish whispered. She grabbed my hand and pulled me to the door. "He's been signaling like this for the past hour. I know how you are about blue jays, so I wanted you to come here. Can you make him go away? That bird is driving me nuts!"

"Irish, I don't want to go in there. And even if I did I can't, because it's probably locked."

"Cady, it's not locked. There's just a bunch of junk in it. Come on."

We pushed the door open. The bird followed us inside where he perched on a battered old crate. The letters on the crate were faded but I could read the name of a bottling company. The bird hopped on one foot and then the other until he bent his head down and clicked his beak on a book resting on top of a pile of old clothes thrown into the crate. I grabbed the book and used the bottom of my T-shirt to brush the dust off on its cover.

"Achoo!" Irish sneezed and then sneezed again. "Let's get out of here; you can bring the book with you."

She pushed me out the door, followed me, and slammed the shed's door shut. The blue jay had flown out ahead of us which was a good thing because Irish slammed that door so hard I thought her neighbors would be coming over any minute to see who was making so much noise.

"There, better. What is that dusty old book about anyway?"

"It's about shipwrecks of Lake Superior," I replied as I dusted some of the dust off its cover.

"Boring, Cady, boring. I better keep the book, I'll leave it in the house for my mom to put back. She keeps track of everything. Sorry to have dragged you over here just to look at a dumb old book. Look at me, I'm a mess. I'm going inside to get cleaned up before the guys come over. Geez, why would that bird want you to find that old book? Do you think it's a clue or something? I know you're working on another mystery aren't you?"

I looked at her and she looked back at me.

I barely had time to mutter, "Maybe," before the blue jay flew down and landed on the book's cover. He tilted his head and looked at me and squawked. Strange, that squawking sounded like, "Clue, clue."

I told myself that birds don't talk. Once again, I asked myself, what was happening.

9 ⚡ Atseknegen (Room)

Later that day, after supper, I watched a game show on television with my Dad until 8 p.m., when I told him I was turning in for the day.

"Kind of early for you, Cady, isn't it? I'll see you in the morning at breakfast."

He rumpled the magazine in his hand, turned its pages, and once again became engrossed in a news story about the state of the world.

I liked my bedroom. The walls were painted white with purple undertones, and a big white paper lantern covered the overhead light fixture. My grandma's handmade patchwork quilt fit my bed perfectly. She used the log cabin pattern in each of the squares and made it using my favorite colors—purple, navy blue, green and white. I plopped down on the bed and switched on the reading lamp.

When I looked up, I noticed the newest thing I'd added to my room. One day last fall, when visiting Grandma, we had gone for a walk in the woods behind her house. I'd found an empty wasp's nest hanging on one of the lower branches of an apple tree, and she told me it was okay to take it. Grandma helped me take it down from the branch.

She handed it to me she said, "Don't worry, it's empty. The old ones taught us to hang an empty nest in the corner of a room. If you sit there and gossip, it will catch the bad words and to prevent your words from hurting anyone."

"Kind of like when a dream catcher catches our bad dreams?" I asked her.

"Yes, something like that."

That evening she showed me how to make dragonflies out of paper and silk.

"When you get home, find a branch to hang from the ceiling in your room. Attach the nest to the branch, and then place these dragonflies around it. This is a good reminder not to sit there gossiping," she told me. She laughed and winked one eye at me. This is just one of the reasons I loved Grandma so much. She made everything happy and fun even when she taught me a lesson.

Tomorrow I'd ask Dad to load more minutes on my phone. Once that was done, I'd call Grandma and ask her about Old Joe.

* * *

I woke up to the fragrant smell of hot oatmeal. Even though it was only late summer, I loved the smell of anything with pumpkins, and dad had loaded it with pumpkin spices and cinnamon.

I skipped my usual shower and pulled on an old pair of jeans and my favorite tie-dyed purple and blue T-shirt and pounded down the stairs and burst into the kitchen.

"What's your hurry, kid? There's plenty for everyone," Dad said. He stood at the counter where he'd taken the lid off the crockpot and stirred the oatmeal.

"I thought maybe Colson would like to try a little even though I know most of it will end up on the floor and smeared all over his face. What about you? A big bowl as usual?"

I nodded and reached for the bowls of almonds and dried cranberries we kept next to the stove. Then I asked about calling Grandma, as planned.

"You know the rules, Cady. Phone calls are only for emergencies. I guess it's okay just this once to call your Grandma. I know you miss her, and I've noticed how hard you're trying to follow the curfews I've given you. Tell her hello for me."

"So, when will you do it?" I couldn't help it, I kept prodding him even though I knew he hated it.

"You're in luck. I'm heading out on errands in a bit. You can watch Colson. I'll stop at the store and have some more minutes put on your phone. You can call your grandma later this afternoon. Don't wait too long; tonight is her bingo night!" and then he actually chuckled.

What was going on? Why was my dad in such a good mood? Weird, but I liked it, especially when I thought of how we used to fight with each other and how I used to end up grounded almost all the time. Back then I didn't think I'd ever be allowed out of the house again. Things started to change when we moved here. Maybe it was because I had started to change since I wanted to set a good example for my little brother.

Crash! Colson pushed his little yellow bowl of oatmeal off the tray of his highchair and started to cry. I wiped the oatmeal off his face and gave him a graham cracker. Oatmeal was flowing everywhere! After he'd eaten the cracker, I washed his face and hands and plopped him behind the gated-off part of the living room where he could play with his toys and not hurt himself or run away. I then cleaned up the kitchen and poured myself a second glass of orange juice.

The next few hours dragged. Francine came home about 12:30 p.m., early again. I guess doughnut sales were slow today. Then Dad came home a few minutes later. He handed me my phone and I raced up the stairs to my bedroom. I didn't mean to slam the door as loud as I did, and he yelled at me to stop it.

"Sorry, it just slammed by itself. I didn't do it on purpose. Honest," I yelled back, then whispered, "I'm sorry."

10 ⚹ Mezodanek (Family)

The phone rang about eight times before Grandma picked it up.

"Sorry, Cady, I was in the backyard and left my phone in the house. Is everything okay?" I could hear Rez Radio playing pow wow music in the background and the wooden shutters outside the kitchen window swinging back and forth in the breeze. They made a creaking noise. These sounds reminded me of all the happy times I'd spent visiting her.

"Yes, Grandma, we're all fine. I want to talk to you about something. Did you ever know anyone called Old Joe?"

Suddenly everything went quiet. A minute or two later I heard her draw in her breath.

"Old Joe? Who told you about him?"

"John Ray asked me to help him dig something up in this yard in back of an old deserted house on the other side of town. He wouldn't tell me what we were digging for until we actually found it."

"It? What did you find?"

"A beautiful old birchbark box with a little journal inside. John Ray thought Old Joe had buried it there."

"So," she said and started to chuckle, "another mystery has found you and that blue jay. Has he been around lately?"

"Uh, yeah, he pecked at my window the day John Ray and I went digging."

"Cady, you know how it goes. When a mystery comes to you in this way, it's your job to solve it. You've been behaving so much better lately. I think this is why you've been rewarded with another challenge to solve."

"Rewarded? This mystery keeps me thinking about it all the time. It's driving me nuts. This is my reward?"

I heard Grandma chuckle and then laugh loudly. I closed my eyes, and I could picture her eyes crinkling up and how she'd rub her stomach when amused about something or when she's happy.

"Yes, Cady, rewarded. Now, as for Old Joe. His life was not an easy one. He was taken to an orphanage when just a baby."

"But John Ray said he was his grandpa's half-brother and his grandpa grew up on the rez."

"Cady, you don't know everything. Sometimes you assume too much. Old Joe had a hard life. He kept running away, I'm not sure he even finished high school. Don't think he was ignorant, he was probably smarter than the rest of us. The janitor at the orphanage took a liking to him. His son had been killed in an accident, and after that, he started to watch out for Old Joe. He taught him how to tinker and fix old engines and motors, how to fix almost anything. He could take things apart and put them back together like nobody's business. As he got older, people started asking for him to fix their cars, their furnaces, basically anything they had."

"He was sort of happy at the orphanage?"

"Let's just say he made the best of it until he ran away. He'd done pretty well there until the janitor took sick and died when Old Joe was only sixteen or seventeen-years-old, then he got sick himself. Maybe pneumonia? I'm not sure what made Joe sick enough to stay in the hospital for a week or two. That was when his dark brown hair turned white. It wasn't until he met Rose when his hair turned back to dark brown. The two of them got married, and Old Joe found a good job as a mechanic. They lived with Rose's folks until they saved enough to buy their own place."

"Grandma, that's a sad story with a little bit of a happy ending."

"Yes, Cady, a happy ending for a long time until it changed."

"What happened next?"

"It will have to be a story for another day. I've got to get ready to go to bingo."

My minutes were almost used up on the phone, so I thanked Grandma and told her I loved her.

"I know you do, little one, and now another adventure begins for you. Let me know what you find out. Oh, and Cady…"

"Yes, Grandma."

"You might brush up on studying beadwork patterns again, because sometimes those patterns are repeated in quill work. Remember, Cady, things will work out in their own time."

"Wait, what…?

She didn't hear me. She'd already ended our phone conversation. Great, another mystery to solve inside of a bigger mystery.

11 ⚡ Jiman (Boat)

I think our school principal was a bit flustered. Last year he'd scheduled ceremonies every Monday morning to start the week. After we went to our homerooms for attendance, the principal would make an announcement. Then we'd go with our class to the gym where all of us—students, teachers, classroom aides, janitors, bus drivers, lunchroom cooks—would stand in one giant circle. An elder would speak, teaching us a lesson or telling us about something he'd seen us do. He'd tell us to behave well during the week and to try our hardest at our studies. He'd hold an oversized abalone shell in one hand and would light cedar, sweetgrass, or sage for smudging.

I'd grown up with my dad smudging at home so I knew about it. However, some new kids at our school were confused. So, the elder usually reminded us we were smudging to remove the negativity from ourselves and from all around us. The elder would light the sage stick or braid of sweetgrass and fan the smoke with an eagle feather. One of the boys helped him.

They'd stand in front of us, one by one, and we'd fan the smoke over us from our head down to our toes. My dad taught me people should take off their glasses when smudging, "so the Creator will know who you are." Not everyone did. Some people left their glasses on and others took them off. I loved how fragrant the air smelled afterward. I'd get so caught up in the ceremony, I'd have to pinch myself to remind me to say *megwetch* (thank you) afterward.

If the girls or women were on their moon time, they were reminded to stand outside of the circle. They were powerful at this time and no one ever teased them or made fun of them for doing this. Rather, the boys and men respected them.

We'd started school on a Tuesday. I think this threw off the principal's schedule. And then some kids showed up who hadn't enrolled ahead of time, which drove the office secretaries nuts according to what I overheard in the hallway. So, it wasn't until Wednesday when we had our first morning ceremony in the gym. John Ray's grandpa waited there for us, leaning on his walker. He smiled at me, and when I smiled back, I noticed his faded T-shirt. I could still see the pattern. It was the same quillwork pattern as on the birchbark box from John Ray! And, it was the same pattern I'd seen on a piece of beadwork at my Grandma's and on one of her aprons!

Then something strange happened. Because it was one of the first days in September and warm in the gym, someone had propped the door open. That pesky blue jay flew into the gym, landed on the rim of the basketball hoop, and then swiveled his head and looked at all of us. He made a loud screeching cry, *jaay-jaay*, and then flew back out the door, an ending to our school year opening ceremonies.

"That's all folks," the principal announced. "Proceed in an orderly fashion to your homerooms. The school day has now begun."

The other kids were busy showing off new school clothes as we filed out of the gym. Didn't they think it strange a bird flew into the gym, looked us over and flew back out outside? But no one else even mentioned it.

I had a feeling, school would be a lot better this year. For one thing, I wouldn't be the new kid because I'd been a student here last year. This year there were other new kids walking down the halls now. I asked myself if I'd looked as lost and scared as some of these kids did. I hated to admit I'd probably looked the same, like a frightened little rabbit trying to act tough.

"Hey, move it," someone shouted at me and shoved me in the back with a book.

"What the...?"

Then I heard her laughter and caught a whiff of strong perfume. I knew Irish was closing in on me.

"I think you overdid the perfume thing today, Irish," I told her.

"Hey, don't blame me. My little brother, weird Georgie, thought it funny to spray me with some old cologne he found in the bathroom. The bus was out in front of our house, I didn't have time to wash it off. Wait till I get home tonight, I'll get even with him."

I didn't ask for details. The last time Irish wanted to get back at Georgie she'd threatened to put dish soap in the goldfish bowl.

When the poor kid imagined his four goldfish floating at the top of the tank, he started to cry. Irish told Georgie that's how you clean a fish tank.

"I didn't do it because, hey, you've got to respect life. Right? Because that respect for life is a basic teaching. I learned that in culture class with you. But it stopped him from playing pranks for a while," she confided. I was glad she didn't actually do it because sometimes Irish could go too far.

"Come on, Cady, I'll show you where my locker is this year."

"Show me after our next class, or I'll be late to history class. Our teacher is our soccer coach, so I don't want to start off on his bad side."

Just then the warning bell rang and as I raced down the hall to my class I heard her yell, "Later 'gator. And you'd better tell me what you dug up with John Ray the other night. I want details. Hear me? I want DETAILS!"

I think the whole school heard her, but that's Irish, my best friend. She crashes through life making a lot of noise while doing it.

* * *

Our history teacher, Dwight Jones, was a big guy who also taught Drivers Ed at our school. He went through college on a football scholarship and told us he'd once worked as a bodyguard for a famous person. All this meant the kids in class listened to him, or pretended they were listening, when he talked to us. Even those friends of Irish, James and Derek, paid attention. Mr. Jones started class by telling us how he expected us to behave in his classroom. He explained the consequences if we didn't. Then he handed out our textbooks.

I opened the book to the first Chapter, I couldn't believe it! My heart started racing, I felt beads of sweat start to form on my forehead when I read the Chapter title, "Shipwrecks of Lake Superior." A drawing of an old ship took up half the page. Flags flew from the ship's deck.

"Okay, class," Mr. Jones began. "We're starting history class this year with a story about something that happened a long time ago not too far north from here, and it affected people you might have heard about.

"The *Delphine Marie* carried iron ore and some called it the pride of the Great Lakes. It was a lot newer and nicer than most of the other ships sailing on Lake Superior, so the merchant sailors were happy when they saw their names on the *Delphine Marie's* ship-out lists. They knew the food would be good and the sleeping quarters comfortable.

"Well, according to what I've been able to find on the Internet and poking around in the library, the *Delphine Marie* was built in the late 1940s. She left Superior, Wisconsin on Nov. 13, 1976, bound for Detroit, Michigan. She was carrying a load of iron ore to the steel mills there. The auto factories in Detroit needed steel to build their cars because they didn't use fiberglass like they do today.

"Everything was great when the ship set sail. It measured four hundred and twenty-seven feet long, about fifty feet at its widest point, and had a depth of twenty-eight feet. Does anyone know what 'depth' means?" he asked us.

No, one knew, so he answered for us and wrote the definition on the whiteboard.

"A ship's depth is the vertical distance from the lowest point of the hull to the deck level. Lake Superior is the largest of the Great Lakes. It's 383 miles long and 160 miles at its widest point. Even a good swimmer would have trouble on the lake because it's 1,333 feet at its deepest. We've got a lot of places around here with French names including this lake. It gets its name from the French, Le Lac Superieur, or Upper Lake."

This next part got most of us sitting up and paying attention.

"Did you ever hear the saying, 'Superior never gives up her dead?'

"There's a book in our school library called *Shipwrecks of the Great Lakes* by Paul Hancock, and in it he explains why the lake doesn't give up her dead. It's because the lake's 'cold temperatures prevents bacterial growth needed to cause the body to float to the surface. In many cases, bodies sink to the bottom, never to be found.'"

I started getting chilled and felt a small shiver run through my body. I looked at Irish and even she shrugged her shoulders nervously.

Mr. Jones paced around the room, waving his arms up and down.

"The men aboard were probably talking about what they'd do when they got to the city. A few thunderstorms and high winds had been predicted. The ship's captain probably figured they could beat the weather. They planned to cross Lake Superior and make it to the Soo Locks in Sault Ste. Marie, Michigan, and from there they'd make their way on Lake Huron traveling south along the eastern side of the Lower Peninsula. About halfway across Lake Superior, the lake's waters started to change. The wind blew at gale force, making waves as high as thirty-five feet.

"It was the worst storm to occur on the Great Lakes in more than fifty years. There were other ships on the lake that day that made it to shelter but not the *Delphine Marie*. Her captain held fast and tried to ride out the storm, then water started to pour into the ship's hold because the hatch covers failed," Mr. Jones said.

He looked at us and noticed our confusion.

"A ship's hold is the space below deck for storing cargo and its hatches are the openings on deck giving access to the hold. Got it?" he asked us.

I couldn't believe how in awe Mr. Jones seemed of this terrible storm. The sadness he felt for the ship's drowned crew showed on his face. I thought I even saw him wipe his left eye with his fist. Sometimes I forget teachers have feelings just like kids.

Leon raised his hand and then blurted out, "You make it sound like it just happened yesterday."

"Well, Leon, to me it's like it did. Growing up around here you hear a lot of stories about the Great Lakes. Anyway, the *Delphine Marie* sank later that day somewhere near Wilson Point, Michigan. She went down so fast none of its men had time to even get on the radio for help. No one survived. To this day, nobody knows exactly happened."

"What do you think happened?" Leon asked.

"No one knows for sure. Maybe the ship started taking on water, that water got to the engine, causing it to break down. Chances are the ship couldn't be steered and became dead in the water and at the mercy of the wind and the currents. It could have hit something else, causing even more damage and taking on more water. We just don't know."

I watched Mr. Jones shake his head as he finished the story.

"That's terrible!" I said almost shouting out the words. Some of the kids I knew had fathers and uncles who sailed on the ore ships on the Great Lakes. A long time ago I even had some cousins who'd sailed on them. My dad's four brothers were Navy veterans. And I loved the water so much—I had learned to swim when I wasn't much older than Colson. My dad used to joke I was part fish and had been born with gills!

"Why didn't they get into the lifeboats?" Leon asked. I could hear the indignant tone in his voice at the thought of so many men dying in the storm and with so little warning.

"Such a good question," Mr. Jones replied.

"Because I wondered about it myself, I did some research. I found the answer in another book in the library, written by a man who studies shipwrecks for a living and then writes about them. The book said the *Delphine Marie* was one of the first ships to sink that carried metal lifeboats. Before, they'd been made of wood.

"When her crew needed to use the lifeboats, they couldn't pry them loose from where they were stored. The lifeboats were stuck in the racks holding them. In the panic and confusion caused when the ship started to sink, the sailors couldn't get them loose. They were supposed to use the davits, which are small cranes used to lower the lifeboats. Unfortunately, they'd rusted solid because they weren't maintained.

"They didn't have the old wooden boats on board. They only had the new metal ones, and they had rusted into the racks as if they'd been welded onto the side of the ship. The crew was young. Most of those twenty-nine guys on board were in their twenties or early thirties.

"The crew probably felt safe because the ship was so new and maybe they forgot to check the lifeboats. Ships like the *Delphine Marie* had a reputation for never sinking. The crew didn't count on a storm with record high waves. They probably wouldn't have survived it even if they had gotten into the lifeboats. Sort of makes sense. Right, class?"

And once again, Leon spoke in his deep, loud voice. I'm guessing all of us could hear his uncertainty. "What you're saying is those poor guys on board never had a chance?"

"Pretty much. I think most of them knew they were in trouble. Think about it. They were taking on a lot of water, and it all happened so fast. Most of those guys probably shipped out for months each year. I'm guessing they felt the storm coming before it hit. It roared at them bigger than they expected. What do you do then? You bail and you pray, and maybe, just maybe you try and make a deal with someone or something. This is what I've figured out."

He looked each one of us in the face as he uttered those final words. They were just starting to sink in when the bell rang.

"To be continued," he told us and waved us out the door.

12 ⚡ Skongemek (School)

Last year I had culture class in the morning, but this year it's my last class of the day. I like culture class because we study our native language and learn more about our traditions. I wasn't the best at beadwork, but I could sketch patterns better than almost anyone else, which made me feel good. I was excited when the bell rang, history class ended and it was time to move down the hall for culture class.

Our teacher told us since it was the first day of school and the last class of the day, she would do something different to start off the semester. Her classroom sat at the end of a long hallway. After we sat down and she'd taken attendance, she stood and said, "Follow me and keep it quiet."

She could be fierce if you upset her, so we did as she told us. She was only five feet, four inches tall. She demanded our respect, and she received it. She was probably in her early forties. Stocky, with broad shoulders, she wore glasses. She never wore makeup.

"I know about dressing, but I'm not talking about high fashion. I'm talking about dressing a deer and I can cook an awesome dressing to serve with it!" she liked to joke. She almost always wore khaki pants and long-sleeved men's shirts buttoned up to the top. Her feet were tiny, and she wore white running shoes unless it was winter when she switched to brown lace-up boots.

"I'm half and half—half Potawatomi and half Chippewa or Ojibway, making me a real 'Potato Chip!'" When she laughed her eyes crinkled up and we all laughed with her no matter how many times she told us this same joke.

Barrel-chested, she wore her thin brown hair straight, and it flowed down past her shoulders. She liked to wave her hands in the air when she talked.

"In case you're wondering, I consider myself a traditional. I follow the old ways. The only reason I'm wearing khakis and not a long skirt is because I have health problems, and wearing pants is easier. When I dance in the arena, I wear my jingle dress and wave my eagle feather fan with pride."

She shared with us her viewpoints about beadwork, recipes, birds, her pet racoon and the bear she chased from her back porch.

"Follow me," she barked after she'd taken attendance.

There were about fifteen of us in class and we stood and followed her down the hallway and waited while our teacher went into the school's main office and signed us out. She then took us outdoors where we walked down the half-mile school driveway onto a back road. Freedom! A dense forest of birch trees on either side of the road surrounded us. We joked and kidded with each other and rejoiced at this unexpected gift of being let loose a bit early for a group walk into the woods around the school. Iris knew we were not used to sitting still after the long summer days of not having class.

"You guys need to move and walk around. While we're outdoors I want you looking at all you see. Remember it. I'll test your recall tomorrow when I'll reinforce it with some traditional teachings."

A few minutes later Mike jabbed me with his elbow and said, "Look, it's a dead porcupine. Too bad, it looks like it's been here a while, so it's too late to take the quills. My mom would have liked them."

Okay, this was getting weird. First John Ray had asked me to help him dig in a deserted yard, and we'd dug up a birchbark box with quillwork. And now Mike told me his mother excelled at quillwork. I'd never even thought about quillwork before, and now it came into my life several times in the past few days.

"*Jaay, jaay, jaay,*" of course, a long day of school would end with that noisy blue jay following me and flapping his wings. I looked up and saw him perched on the branch of a nearby birch tree. Can birds wink? Because I'm sure he winked at me. My pulse started to race because of all the signs coming to me. I'd be glad to get on the bus and go home. I needed some quiet time in my bedroom to try to figure out all of this.

* * *

I rode the same bus home as last year with the same bus driver, Gus. He kept law and order on his bus, and nobody fooled around or they'd have to answer to him. Also, we had cameras on the bus—and they actually worked and recorded everything.

Gus gave us the same opening-week speech as he did last year.

"Listen up. You can talk on my bus, but I'd rather you just put your headphones on and listen to whatever you listen to. No foolishness, and I mean no foolishness—which means no fighting, no bullying, no throwing things. Got it? And just in case you haven't 'got it,' those cameras overhead do 'get it.' And they work. I only drive bus as a break from my real job, which is fixing lawn mowers and chainsaws and stuff. Are there any questions? No? Good, then let's go."

Half an hour later Gus dropped me off at home. On the way up the stairs to my room, I forgot Dad's rules about not slamming doors and the wind caught the door as I opened it and—boom! It made a loud noise, causing my baby brother to cry.

"Cady, that better be you and it better be an apology I hear," Dad's voice thundered out at me.

"Sorry, sorry," I muttered even though I really wasn't feeling very sorry. I made sure to stomp my feet as I went to my room until I remembered to not get so mad all the time. Sometimes it's so hard to behave myself and follow rules, but I made sure not to slam my bedroom door.

I don't think grownups realize how hard it is to follow all the rules they give us. The thinking part of me says they're made for a good reason and probably to protect us. Sometimes, it's just a lot to make myself do. I don't lose my temper and explode as much as I used to—even though I still get angry a lot of the time. I'm better at keeping my anger to myself. Running helps. Also, now that I have a baby brother in the house, I can see how he needs rules because they keep him safe. He's just a little guy who doesn't know that sticking things into electrical outlets could hurt him or that an open door to the basement could be dangerous. He wants to go exploring but if he fell down the stairs he could get hurt. I don't even like to think about those things.

All this thinking after the excitement of a new school year wore me out. I flopped on my bed. I started to squish my head into my favorite pillow when I felt something stabbing my back.

"What the...?"

It was the book about quillwork I'd found last night. I rested the book on my stomach and started leafing through the pages until page seventy-six. And then I found it—the pattern I'd seen on John Ray's grandfather's shirt, on my grandma's apron, and on the lid of the birchbark box!

This time I looked more closely at the pattern. I'd looked at it before. but I hadn't studied it. Whoever had designed it used several patterns, and they all worked together. I liked it because you had to look carefully to absorb its perfection.

A large circle formed its background, and the quills in it were white. Then, two bands crossed it, forming an X and they were brown. Green leaves surrounded the pinecone in its center. The best part? Inside each of the legs of the X were stars and feathers forming a pattern of star, feather, star, feather, etc. The stars were yellow, the feathers red and black. What did this mean? Or did it mean anything? I wanted to ask my grandma, but I didn't want to ask her during a phone call because I remembered something she'd told me many years ago.

"I hope we've taught you some things are best talked about in face to face, Cady."

I wouldn't see her for a few weeks until she came here for a visit. My friends wouldn't know. John Ray might but he wasn't here. Would there be a book at the library? Our school library was also was the tribal library and had lots of books about native history. Our librarian was Ojibwa and I hoped she could help me.

I started to write my questions down when I heard Dad calling us for dinner. I closed the book and went downstairs.

* * *

We had another one of my dad's favorite meals for dinner that night because it was easy to make. "Yup, this is an old Army recipe. I've cut the ingredient measures down for our family. I'm not cooking for two hundred anymore," he told us and actually smiled.

It smelled amazing—meatloaf with gravy, mashed potatoes, hot rolls with butter and honey and corn on the cob.

"Dig in, don't be shy. We're celebrating tonight."

I must have looked confused because he actually seemed to chuckle.

"It's no big secret. Last year I worked part-time hours at the reservation, with no set schedule. I have big news—my contract has been extended, which means I'll be teaching our language at the rez's cultural center for the next few months."

I was happy for my dad because preserving our language is probably the most important thing in the world to him. I know he loves all of us, but sometimes I think he loves the language more. I've gotten used to asking him a question and then waiting for the longest time before he answers me.

"I don't think in English, Cady. It takes me a few minutes to gather my thoughts and then answer you in English," he'd tell me and then bug me about learning our native language. Back then it didn't seem important to me but I'm older now and starting to learn more about my culture. I decided I'd try a little harder. And then it hit me. Dad would be working just down the road from the school.

I didn't know if I liked the idea because I liked having my space and getting away from home. Would he be dropping in at school to check on me?

13 ⋆ Jigatek (By Trees)

After Culture Class the next day, our teacher asked me to stay behind.

"Hold on a moment, Cady, I've got a message for you from John Ray's grandma. She'd like you to come over today; she's got something to tell you. School's done for the day. You could scoot over there now, it's close enough to walk."

"I can't. I have to be on the bus, or my dad will get mad. And Gus, the bus driver, will get mad if I'm late and make him wait."

"It's okay, I've cleared it with both of them. I guess you didn't know Gus is my cousin. I've called your Dad, and he's called the office to tell them you won't be on the early bus. You can catch the five o'clock bus into town with the rest of the kids who stay late for after-school tutoring."

She handed me a book and added, "Here, give this to Grandma Eunice when you get there. I borrowed it from her and she needs it back. Now scoot." She waved her hand to send me on my way. I knew she just wanted me to leave, then she could open the bottle of soda she kept in her desk. Teachers weren't allowed to have soda in their rooms because they were told it set a bad example for the students. Everyone knew how much she loved her soda. She stood up and started fidgeting and moving her feet in a dance pattern. I knew I'd better get out of there.

Funny how they do things out here. It sure isn't like my old school back in Minnesota. Everyone here seems to be related to everyone else or to know them really well. I kind of like it even though the bad part is everyone knows everyone else's business. This is my second year here, and I'm still getting used to it.

I grabbed my backpack from my locker and made sure I had my sketchbook, some pencils and my trusty old beat-up, yet reliable, cell phone. I didn't know why John Ray's grandma wanted to see me. I couldn't stop fidgeting and hunching my shoulders and then moving them around some more. She was John-Ray's grandma, not mine. Even though she was a family friend, she was an elder, and I didn't know her very well.

Kids were racing out the front doors of the school and lining up for the three buses in front. There were two adults supervising them and making sure each kid got on the right bus. Sometimes the little kids got confused and might end up on a bus going south when they should have been on the one going north into Barnesville. I started walking to John Ray's grandma's house when I heard Gus hollering at me, "It's okay, Cady. I'll pick you up later," before he waved me away.

I straightened up my backpack on my shoulders and headed off down the road to my destination, about a half-mile from school. Because it was about three-thirty in the afternoon, the sun warmed the air. I wore my favorite washed out and faded black jeans and an old T-shirt of Bruce's. He collected T-shirts from 1980s heavy metal bands, and gave me one for my birthday each year. He called it vintage and "way cool." I was glad I wore my second favorite pair of running shoes, the blue and silver ones, and not my black ankle boots. It wasn't a long walk, but because I was wearing running shoes, I could jog down the road.

I heard clear whistling notes and looked up at the trees towering over the road. The blue jay circled over me and it looked like he wanted to lead the way for me.

The trees had started to turn colors and their leaves showed in brilliant shades of red and gold and brown. The slight breeze felt deliciously cool as it brushed across my face. I liked the sound the wind made when it rustled through the branches.

That noise again. Then I heard a stone drop and roll on the road in front of me.

I thought of a poem our culture teacher read to us in class last year, titled "Nature Sounds." It spoke about listening to the wind. I'd forgotten most of it, but I'd written down two lines afterward and memorized them: "Listen to the wind," she told her students on a cold day in January. "We can learn so much from the trees and the sound it made, like *si-si-gwa-d*, rushing through it."

"What the...?" That pesky blue jay flew overhead as if leading the way for me. Had the bird dropped the stone to get my attention? And how could a bird drop a stone anyway? Don't birds use their beaks to dig up seeds and worms—not stones? Once again, I felt as if my head was starting to spin.

14 ⚡ Koye (Grandmother)

I stood on the porch of John Ray's grandma's house. Some loose dirt from the road had wedged in the ridges on the bottom of my shoes. I rubbed my shoe on the porch's doormat, trying to shake it loose when the front door flew open.

"Oh, for goodness sake, Cady. Don't worry about a little dirt, come on in," Grandma Eunice said in greeting me. "If your shoes are dirty, you can take them off and leave them on the doormat."

"Uh, okay," I told her. I slipped off my shoes and padded in my socks into the living room.

Wonderful smells of baking bread scented the air, and my stomach rumbled a bit.

I hadn't eaten much at lunch today because I didn't like what they were serving—mac and cheese and fish sticks. Most kids love that stuff, but I don't. My dad's cousin, Liddie, my favorite cook at school, had called in sick. She usually gives me something special on macaroni and cheese days, like leftover chili or lasagna, or she'd make a chef's salad for me. A substitute cook worked for her in the kitchen today. I had to settle for what I could find— carrot sticks, crackers and an apple. Even this morning's yogurt bin was empty.

"It's because it's been a busy day, today, Cady," Jane, another cook told me. "We had a lot of community members come in for to-go boxes, and we're pretty much wiped out of food. Sorry about that, kiddo."

High school kids had the very last lunch period of the day, after the Day Care and elementary school kids. Community members could come in at noon and get super-inexpensive "to go" boxes, and sometimes I saw people leave carrying two or three or even six boxes. Sometimes by the time we got there it was twenty minutes past noon and everything was pretty much picked over. Today had been one of those days.

My stomach gurgled and rumbled when I heard John Ray's grandma's voice interrupting my daydreams.

"Just a minute, I'll be right back. I've got something I want to show you," she said interrupting my thoughts about food. "Would you like some banana bread and a glass of lemonade?"

"Yes, *megwetch*," I said, and she must have liked my answer because she laughed out loud. "Go in the kitchen and help yourself; I've left it out for you on the table. I'll be right back." Her long cotton skirt swayed around her legs as she walked down a hallway. Her skirt was dark blue with a pattern of tiny red and yellow flowers on the top part. I liked John Ray's grandmother a lot because she reminded me of my grandmother. They both walked gracefully and wore their long, gray hair pinned in a bun at the back of the neck. And they both liked to cook and wear dangling earrings. John Ray's grandma wore beaded earrings each time I saw her.

The earrings dangled from delicate wires poked through her earlobes. A tiny bear sat at the top of each earring, made in the new style of turquoise jewelry—its colors were turquoise, dark green, yellow, red and brown. Each color was sharply outlined in black like a stained-glass window. Two tiny silver balls and one copper one hung underneath and a cowry shell dangled at the bottom.

I had been taught that in the "old days," in some tribes, a woman's jewelry showed how much her family valued her, especially if it was silver. This was why I was excited when Francine took me to get my ears pierced a few months ago. Maybe someday I would wear beautiful earrings like Grandma Eunice and my own Grandma Winnie.

I was sitting at Grandma Eunice's kitchen table eating banana bread and drinking a glass of lemonade when she sat down next to me.

"I see you like my banana bread. I've always felt teenagers need fuel to help them through their growth spurts. Have another piece; there's another loaf cooling on the shelf."

"Yes, ma'am. Thank you." I helped myself to another piece of bread and poured a second glass of lemonade.

"It's good to see a young girl with a healthy appetite. Glad you're not one of those girls who is always fretting about her weight. Here, this is what I've brought to show you," she added. She pointed to a birchbark box like the one John-Ray and I had dug up. I couldn't believe it.

"There's actually another one just like this out in the world somewhere, probably buried," she told me. She looked at me as if we shared a secret, and then she winked at me.

"This box belonged to one of my dearest friends, Rose. Before she married Joe, she made those boxes to celebrate their wedding. She gave one to Joe and she kept one for herself. We were not much more than kids when she made these. Her family lived out in the country." These must have been good memories for her because she started smiling.

"Well, it used to be in the country, now it's part of the reservation. During the last few years, the tribe has been able to buy back parcels of land and add to the reservation's size.

"Rose liked all of our traditional activities—beadwork, sewing, tanning hides, and fishing. She loved hiking in the woods and learned how to harvest birchbark from some of the old-timers. It wasn't long after that when she began to make birchbark boxes and bowls. And, naturally, since she was artistic, she wanted to learn to decorate them. It didn't cost her money to use quills. Her grandma taught her how to hunt for porcupines and harvest the quills and then prepare them for her designs."

"Is that who taught her how to dye the quills?" I couldn't help asking before realizing I had interrupted her.

"Yes, as well as a few others who wanted to pass on knowledge of the craft. I've got a book or two around here if you'd like to borrow them," she told me.

I nodded. "I'd like that."

"Our lives were pretty quiet back then by today's standards. I sometimes think they were better without all the interruptions of television and computers. Technology has given us some good things, but we have to be careful to hold on to our traditional ways before we lose them completely." She started drumming her fingers on the table and looked away from me and out the window.

"Grandma Eunice, what about the pattern on the boxes and on Abe's little journal and on my grandma's apron?"

"Oh, Cady, that will have to be a story for another day. You better go now. Your bus will be leaving school soon, and you don't want to be late. I'll get those books for you."

I stood up, walked to the doorway, and bent down to tie my shoes. As I looked up she handed me the books. I put them in my backpack.

"Oh, I almost forgot. John Ray sent this to you." She handed me a postcard from North Dakota. The front showed a mountain range, on the back he'd written "Making any progress?"

"*Bama pi*, little one," she said which means "until we meet again."

"*Bama pi*," I replied and took off running to catch my bus. I tried hard not to be mad. I wanted to learn things but when I asked adults (and I asked respectfully), they would tell me, "A story for another day." Why did they hold on to their secrets?

15 ⚹ Bmadzewen (Life)

As if I didn't have enough to think about—soccer games, the mystery of Old Joe and the quillwork box and little journal—another surprise came to me. Mr. Jones started history class the next day with a startling announcement.

"Okay, class, pay attention. You've got four weeks to complete your next assignment. This project will count for eighty percent of your quarter grade, so it's important. Attendance and a test will count for the rest. Are you listening?"

I was listening even if some of the other kids weren't. I wanted to stay on the soccer team. I was a midfielder on our team, and we were scheduled to play six away games. Coach didn't let us travel to those games unless we carried at least a C average. Sometimes he got tough and demanded a grade point average higher than a C.

I felt a few nervous flutters in my stomach. Writing papers was hard for me: I was much better at sketching. And speaking in front of class? The worst! Some kids liked it. Irish loved being on stage. She bragged it gave her the chance to "strut her stuff." Not me, I liked keeping my head down, thinking my own thoughts and sketching.

"I'm giving you a handout with what's expected," Mr. Jones continued. "Basically, I want you to research a shipwreck on the Great Lakes. There's a lot of information on the internet, and Miss O'Malley in the library is getting some material together. She's on board with this project, and the library can be a great resource for you. Those of you who live in town could also use the Barnesville library. Don't be afraid to ask around and find out who might have sailed on the Great Lakes, because they might have some stories to add."

Derek, Irish's friend, raised his hand.

"It sounds like a lot of work. Don't know if I'm up for it," Derek told the class.

"Yes, Derek, it will be a lot of work, that's why it will count for eighty percent of your quarter grade. Here's the good news. We're going to try something new this year. I don't want you to write the usual five-page research paper. Instead, I'm going to give each of you a spiral-bound notebook, and I want you to write your report in the first person.

You will be keeping a journal and writing as if you were one of the sailors on a ship crossing one of the Great Lakes. You will need to do research for this, no making up facts. This will be a different kind of writing and reporting for you. I've set aside class time, including time in the computer lab, for you to do your research. I've also talked to your English teacher, and she's agreed to give you guys one day a week in her class to work on this with her help. It's very important that you list your references. No cutting and pasting off the Internet. You will need to write what you find into your own words. Have I made myself clear?"

Derek shrugged and muttered, "Yeah, I got it."

A few of the kids laughed because they knew Derek's grandfather was pretty strict. He'd be in trouble if he failed a class. His uncle was one of our school janitors and reported back to the family about Derek's behavior in school. Derek tried to act tough, but it's a hard act to pull off with the way his family kept an eye on him.

"Any questions?"

One or two hands went up. Jennie asked if she could just show a movie about a shipwreck.

"No, absolutely not, but I will allow you to put together a PowerPoint presentation or make your own video for extra credit," Mr. Jones added.

Irish sat in the desk behind me and poked my back. I knew she would be giggling because Jennie had one interest in life—giving herself manicures. She said she liked to practice for the day she had her own salon.

72

"Wonder if she'll make a movie about painting shipwrecks on nails," Irish whispered.

I couldn't help it and burst out laughing.

"Cady Thunder, would you care to tell the class what's so funny about shipwrecks? Personally, I don't think brave people losing their lives on the open water is amusing, I'm surprised you do," Mr. Jones trumpeted. Then he dropped a few pencils on his desk. They made a rattling noise when they landed on the desktop. My shoulders twitched in reaction.

The bell rang signaling the end of class.

I stood and blurted, "Sorry," then grabbed the handout, a notebook, and my backpack, and fled the room.

* * *

I begged Dad to let me use his phone that night to call Grandma. After I told him I needed to talk to her about my history assignment, he relented (another of my new words— relent, which means to make less severe) and told me I could have twenty minutes.

"No more than that. I paid for those minutes, I don't want you using them up," he said as if he had to explain. Dad had gotten in trouble over a cellphone bill a few years ago, and after that he bought minutes. He didn't have a fancy phone, just one he bought at the dollar store and loaded with minutes.

"I don't need an expensive phone, and this way I stay away from running up big bills," he announced every month. We had the internet at home, and because he worked for the reservation, they paid for the monthly charge. We only had one computer; the one dad had won at bingo. He let me use it for school projects. Otherwise, I'd use the ones in the computer lab at school, or the public library in town.

"Okay, Cady, I've set the timer. You can call Grandma now, and tell her I said 'hey.'" Dad handed me his phone, and I got as far away as I could—which meant I sat in an old rocking chair on our front porch.

After Grandma and I chatted a few minutes about the eagles she'd seen nesting in the woods in back of her house, I settled in to ask her my questions.

"Grandma, I've got a history class assignment. It will count for most of my grade this quarter. It's important because I want to keep my place on the soccer team, so I need to earn good grades."

The words flowed from my mouth until grandma interrupted me.

"Hold on, Cady. That was one mighty long sentence. If you're asking me for help, well, of course I'll help you. Cady, you haven't told me what you need."

"Do you know anything about shipwrecks on the Great Lakes? Or anyone who might have been on a shipwreck and who lived through it? You told me you grew up around here, and I hoped you could help me. You're the only one I could think of to ask for help," I told her.

"Cady, Cady, Cady, you always surprise me," she replied and then I heard her wonderful throaty chuckle.

"Your friend John Ray's relative, Old Joe's twin brother, Abe, sailed the Great Lakes for a few years. He's gone now, so sad. I think you should start with learning about the Christmas Tree Ship. Yes, you should start there. You will have many interesting discoveries ahead of you, my girl. How about this? After you start your research you can call me again and fill me in with how it's going. I've got to hang up. My tea kettle is on the stove and about to boil over." Our conversation ended.

Then I did something I used to do when I became nervous. With my right hand, I pinched the little webbed area between my thumb and index finger on my left hand.

It's going to be okay. Grandma's older, but she's on my side. I'll show her Abe's journal. She knows a lot and maybe she can tell me what it means.

Maybe things would be work out with my grandma helping me. Even though she lived in Minnesota and I lived in Michigan we could talk on the phone. And she loved to surprise us with visits. Books and websites could tell me a lot but some things were passed down from the elders to the next generations. What did she know about Old Joe and what did she know about shipwrecks?

Great, another mystery. Only I didn't think it was great.

Abe. His name started to come up when we talked about Old Joe. Grandma had just said Abe and Joe were twin brothers! Did other people know this? My head spun with this new information. I poured myself a glass of apple cider and grabbed a handful of pretzels from an open bag on the kitchen counter that I took up the back staircase to my bedroom.

This time I slammed the door!

16 ⚹ Gwdekto (He Struggles)

"What is happening?" I asked myself this question over and over. Everything was going so well...until it wasn't. Couldn't anything ever work out? And why couldn't things in my life work out for me at the same time? Just when it seemed my life started to calm down at home, things fell apart everywhere else.

Irish was mad at me. I could still hear her voice when she'd shrieked at me today when I walked down the hall. I raced out of our school building's front doors and ran outside. I boarded my bus and started muttering to myself. Thirty minutes later we were about ten blocks from our house and only Gus, the driver, and me were left.

"Okay, kiddo, what's up? What's got you so upset?" Gus asked me. He looked at me in the rearview mirror, and his mouth curved a bit until it almost resembled a smile.

"You wouldn't understand, Gus."

"Kid, I've been driving this bus for twenty years. There's nothing I haven't heard."

"It's good, Gus, I'll figure it out. Thanks for asking."

Silence reigned for the next ten minutes until Gus hollered, "Hey, Cady, look at the sign." He drove the bus past a hardware store on the outskirts of town and pointed at it.

"Read the sign. It says 'Apples, Corn, Beets, Ammo.' Only in the Upper Peninsula, only in the UP," and he shook his head. I don't pay much attention to hardware store signs even though Gus seemed very excited about this one.

He pulled the bus up in front of our house. I loved the sounds the bus made as it stopped. The brakes squeaked and whistled. "It's pneumatic, boys," I once heard him tell a few of the boys on our route. I'm not sure what pneumatic means, but it sounded cool. Complicated—but cool.

Gus pulled on the heavy bar to the right of his seat and the door swung open.

"Time to get out, Cady, tell your dad 'hey' from me."

"Sure, Gus, see you tomorrow," I answered back. A few minutes later Gus and his bus disappeared from sight.

Irish was my best friend and I couldn't stand it when she was mad at me. Did she think I broke into her locker and stole her stupid pink glitter backpack? One of her goofy friends probably did it but because the two of us had exchanged locker codes as part of our friendship pact—and now she blamed me.

When Irish was mad she roared.

"Cady Whirlwind Thunder, give me back my backpack now!" she'd yelled at me. Then she stomped her foot down hard.

"Irish, I don't have your stupid backpack. I don't even like pink or glitter or unicorns." She didn't listen to me. She slammed her locker door and ran to the bus.

It got worse. Mr. Jones had assigned each of us our own shipwreck to study, and Irish and I were set to be partners. Two heads are better than one, right? And we'd come up with a brilliant idea. We'd research the Christmas Tree Shipwreck like my grandma had suggested! But now Irish was mad at me, and I didn't know if I wanted to kick something or break down and cry.

The next two days dragged by. Each minute seemed like an hour. I missed Irish and her fun-loving ways. Plus, Colson started to walk and it seemed like he got into everything. I had to watch him if my dad or Francine were busy in another room.

"My baby will not be put in a playpen," Francine told us at dinner that night. "He needs to learn to be independent." She slammed down her spoon to reinforce those words. "Got it?"

Dad nodded. He'd become used to her ways, but I still had to force myself to smile back at her.

"Geez, Francine, I get it. I love the little guy, I'll help watch him." I pushed my chair away from the table and stomped out of the kitchen and upstairs to my bedroom.

Guess I'm living up to my name—wawyasto (Whirlwind).

And then I couldn't help it; the tears came pouring out and were soaking into my favorite yellow pillow, the one Irish had given me on my last birthday.

Clack, clack, clack!

What? The busy bird was back again and clicking his beak against the window. Why couldn't he just leave me alone in my misery? He kept up his racket for another two or three minutes until Dad hollered up the stairs.

"Cady, get down here. Your grandma's on the phone and wants to talk to you. I'm not walking up those stairs again, so you better get down here now!"

I left my room and walked down the stairs, quietly this time, to hear my Dad saying, "Yes, Mother, I understand. Yes, she's a teenage girl, I've been through this before with her older sisters. Cady has got to work on her attitude. Enough is enough."

He turned around and handed me the phone. The look he gave me seemed to say, "Behave yourself," and he walked off.

"Cady, now you're growing up there are some things I need to talk to you about. I plan to visit you soon, and I'll explain more then. And speaking of explorations, how are you doing on your research for your class project?"

"Terrible. Irish was going to be my partner but now she's not talking to me," I spoke through my tears.

"There, there, Cady. These things happen and soon it will straighten out. I promise you. Didn't you see the messenger bird at your window? Good thing I called to cheer you up. I tell you what, I'll help you and be your partner. Would you like to partner with me?"

"That'd be wonderful, but you're not a student. You don't live here, and Dad limits my phone calls and my computer time. How can it work?"

"Cady, let me work it out. Now, let's get started. You mentioned shipwrecks. Have you chosen one yet?"

"Yes, the Christmas Tree Shipwreck like you suggested," I replied and wiped my sleeve across my eyes to dry my tears. I could feel myself starting to calm down. I loved Grandma so much. Why, oh, why, did she have to live so far away?

"Good, that ship had a name—the Rouse Simmons. There's a lot of information available about it, and its story ought to be told more often. That's my bit of wisdom for today."

"*Megwetch*, Grandma; thanks for everything."

"Good night, dear. Remember your Grandma loves you and is here for you."

"*Bama pi,*" I whispered.

17 ∻ Mjegkowe (Friend)

Grandma always made me feel better. My mom had left my dad and me when I was just a little kid. Years later, Dad married Francine. Then they had Colson and now Francine was absorbed in taking care of him. I knew Grandma belonged to me. I knew she cared about me, which meant the world.

If only she lived closer, if only she lived closer.

I hummed to myself, trying to sleep. I was about to doze off when I realized that I hadn't seen the blue jay for days. His last message to me was, "start your research," but I'd ignored it. I had my LIFE to deal with—soccer and school and babysitting. I didn't have time for research even though I knew people were counting on me.

By procrastinating, I thought I was letting the solution come to me. I thought I was letting things solve themselves as they were meant to. But maybe it was time to start doing more? I would give myself a deadline—the school talent show—to solve the mystery of the quill box and its journal. Deep down I knew I needed to use my gift, solving mysteries. But I also knew I couldn't rush things because that could change how they ended. Would setting a deadline hurt the process?

The next morning was Saturday. We were eating breakfast when Dad asked me my plans for the day. I told him I wanted to do some research in the library for my history project.

"Good idea, Cady. The library is only open until 3 p.m. today, and it's already after nine. Once you've showered and are ready, I'll drop you off there, because I've got a few errands to take care of."

I remembered to grab my denim jacket on the way out the door. It was already the third week of school, and the September afternoons were starting to cool. My older brother, Bruce, had given me a denim backpack for my last birthday. He'd added a beadwork medallion he'd made to the front flap.

I liked the design and asked him if it had special meaning.

"Maybe one day we'll talk about it. That will be a story for another day," he replied. Then he'd winked at me and gotten up for another piece of chocolate birthday cake.

I packed my sketchbook, a notebook, some index cards, and a handful of ballpoint pens. I tucked my beat-up old cellphone in the pocket of my jeans.

Dad honked the horn once, which meant I better get moving. I pulled open the passenger side door of his truck and climbed in. He didn't say much on the short ride to the library. When he pulled up at the front door, he handed me a five-dollar bill.

"This is in case you need to make copies. I seem to remember John Ray paid for those last time."

My thoughts moved back to last spring when John Ray had taught me how to use the microfilm machine at the library. He'd paid for the copies and given them to me. He'd also bought me a glass of ginger ale at the coffee shop across the street from the library. I didn't want to think about it today because he wasn't here. I didn't want to think about how much I liked him and how much I missed him. Just before he left, I asked him how he could go to South Dakota when we had school. He'd told me his aunt would home school him.

I shook my head to chase these thoughts away.

Get going, Cady, you have research to do and a mystery to solve. Time enough for thinking about John Ray later.

I wanted to earn an A on this report. I'd promised my family and myself I'd turn over a new leaf when we moved here one year ago. I wanted Dad and Grandma to be proud of me. Because I was on the soccer team, I needed to earn good grades. John Ray told me the coaches were tough about grades and didn't put up with any nonsense. Sometimes I slipped into "nonsense," as John Ray called it, but I was growing up and wanted to walk a good path.

"Thanks, Dad. I mean it, thanks a lot. I'll see you at dinner tonight?"

"You bet. It's twice-baked potatoes and fried chicken night. Gonna be a feast!"

I climbed out of the truck, taking care not to slam the door before Dad drove off. I walked toward the library's entrance and noticed that blue bird perched on a nearby bench.

Click, click, click. Did that bird just say, 'Welcome back, Cady. Welcome back.' Ney, silly girl. He's just a bird, and everyone knows birds don't talk.

"Don't be so sure of it," I heard my grandma say as if she was standing next to me.

Our town's library is famous for its grandfather clock. I love the way it chimes the hours loudly enough to hear throughout the building. It's not annoying because it's so musical and not like that bird clock in the coffee shop across the street where I'd met John Ray for ginger ale. That clock had different types of birds on it which made a different bird sound at each hour. It could be annoying if you didn't like birdsongs. The musical chimes of the grandfather clock in the library were soothing and calming. I liked these sounds better.

I looked up after hearing two loud chimes, musical but booming. What? It was 2 p.m.? I'd been poring through books in the library since before 10 a.m! I'd only stopped to wander outside to eat the oat and honey granola bar I'd found at the bottom of my backpack. It's not my favorite flavor but I was hungry enough to eat anything.

I couldn't believe how much information I'd found about the Christmas Tree Shipwreck. Grandma had been right. It was famous. I checked out one book in the children's section and two others in the adult section about the ship. This project held the promise of something interesting. How did it relate to Old Joe and his family? The years didn't match up. And why was the birchbark box and its little journal so important? And would I ever find out the meaning of the special design in the quillwork?

Grandma had told me to take it one step at a time and not to rush.

"Don't bite off too much at once, Cady. Do what you can, and we'll see what we will see." Then she switched subjects on me, something grown-ups seemed to do a lot. I promised myself I'd be different when I grew up. I'd talk and talk and probably bore kids with my never-ending stories.

I slung my backpack over my shoulders and left the library, walked down our main street and looked in the windows on my way. Dawdle is what Dad would call it. I loved to window shop and could do it for hours. I'd spent three dollars at the library making copies, so I still had two dollars left. I could hear the copies rustling around in my backpack and wondered if two dollars would be enough to buy at least a small bag of caramel corn?

There's a candy store across the street from the library. It's famous for its popcorn and caramel corn. They popped the corn in old heavy iron pots on gas burners and poured melted butter over the popped corn. They didn't use a butter substitute. Irish told me her mom and the owner were friends. The owner had told her mom, "We're practically next door to the dairy state, so I'm using real butter on my popcorn!" The shop didn't look too busy, and I pushed open the door in a hurry.

"Hey, watch it, you almost hit me." I looked up and saw Irish!

"Cady, I'm so sorry," she said and I could hear the tears choking her voice. I looked at the silly pink backpack hanging from her left arm.

"I know you didn't take it. How could I ever have thought so? Stupid Derek stole it from my locker as a joke. I'd shoved the backpack into the locker and slammed the door when the bell rang. I forgot to close the combination lock, and it still hung from the door, so Derek reached in and took my backpack. He said he was looking for contraband. Contraband? I asked him. Like lip gloss or a hair brush? Honestly, he's such a jerk! Can you ever forgive me? Please, please! Tell me you'll forgive me; you're my best friend in the whole wide world."

She stretched out her arms.

"Look. I got paid from my babysitting job. Let me buy you the biggest bag of caramel corn they've got. Oh, Cady, I've missed you so much."

She threw her arms around me for a hug. I watched the clerk put an enormous bag of caramel corn on the counter.

"Forgive me?"

"Sure. I forgive you. What choice do I have?"

We were best friends again. Between the two of us we devoured an entire bag of delicious and sticky caramel corn as we walked home. I couldn't decide what tasted better, having my best friend back or the rich and buttery caramel corn.

18 ⚡ Lac Superieur (French) Lake Superior

After dinner that night Dad quizzed me on what I had found at the library. I'd been talking back to him and Francine more than usual lately. It's something I do when I'm stressed. I was trying to improve. However, sometimes I gave up, and lashed out. I knew I had to try harder to be more respectful. I was a big sister now and I wanted to set a good example for my baby brother.

"I checked out a DVD from the library. It's about some old sailing ships. I'm going to write about the Christmas Tree Shipwreck for my report. I thought I might learn something from watching this. Do you want to watch it with me?"

Every now and then he surprises me.

"Sure, let's watch it after dinner. I think Francine can handle the cleanup tonight. Right, dear?"

"Of course, Ed, no problem."

* * *

The story shown on the DVD was roughly the same as what Mr. Jones had told us in history class. One of the ships wasn't even ten years old when it sank, carrying a full load of iron ore pellets weighing about twenty-five thousand tons. It left Minnesota to travel across Lake Superior to the Port of Detroit.

"Cady, one of the things I teach students in my language class is that some called Lake Superior 'Otchipwe-kitch-gami,' meaning Sea of the Ojibwe people. *Gitchie* means large or big, and *gami* means lake."

I could hear the growing excitement in my dad's voice. He likes to study history and asked if I had taken notes while we were watching the DVD.

"Uh, no, but I have my research from the library." I stood up and grabbed my backpack from where I'd thrown it on the floor earlier in the day. I rummaged around and pulled out the printed sheets and held them out to him.

"No, Cady, I'd rather you read it to me." He tapped his pen against his notebook. It made a *thruck, thruck, thruck* sound as the expression on his face grew serious.

"I found a website called Lake Superior Facts and it said the lake's name is from the French world Lac Superieur which means Upper Lake. It covers 31,700 square miles. There have been 352 shipwrecks on the lake. It's a deep lake, 1,333 feet at its deepest! It has as much water as all the other Great Lakes put together plus three extras the size of Lake Erie!

"And, Dad, they once measured waves 31-feet high! That's as if there were five of you on top of each other. Those men on board the ships must have been so scared when they knew their ship was sinking."

"I agree, Cady. Did you know your grandpa once sailed as a merchant seaman? He only made two trips, but he told me it's possible to have thirty-foot waves when all the conditions are right, especially wind conditions. It's the wind conditions creating the waves."

"How come you never told me Grandpa had been out on one of those big ships?"

"How come you never asked me?" He added a smile, so I knew he wasn't mad. "Now you'll have more to talk about with your grandma when you talk to her again."

And then I couldn't help it, I started to tear up.

"It seems like forever since I've seen her. I never get to see her since we've moved here."

Just then Dad's phone beeped with a text message. He loved to receive texts and emails from folks throughout the country who asked him things about our native language. He'd answer them, and then they'd ask even more questions.

"It's work I enjoy, Cady, because I'm helping to keep our language alive," he once told me.

Looking up from his phone, Dad said, "Enough work for us tonight, Cady. Time for you to turn in now."

I grabbed my backpack and stomped up the stairs.

Learning my grandad had once sailed on a ship made me curious who he'd been. I remembered riding in the car with him as a little girl when he'd told me, "Never point at a hawk, Cady. Never." He never told me why, and I always wondered about it. Was this a superstition, or a traditional native belief? I made a mental note to ask my dad about it.

I had study hall in the computer lab tomorrow, and I would look up superstitions about sailors and shipwrecks. Maybe this information would lead to more about what had happened to Old Joe even though I knew he would have been too young to have sailed on the Christmas Tree Ship. I needed more research for my history journal-writing assignment so I crossed my fingers I'd learn something to help me. I reached over and turned off my bedside lamp, punched my pillow down and fell asleep.

* * *

One of my teachers had called in sick, and they couldn't find a sub for her. It meant I got to spend an extra half hour in the computer lab absorbed (another cool word I liked to use which means to take in and understand fully) in my research. I thought back to last spring when John Ray had helped with my research about the antique necklace by showing me how to use the microfilm machine at the public library.

Enough of your daydreaming, Cady, get back to work.

I looked up at the clock and then at the aide who was supervising us in the lab. Yup, it was definitely time to get serious. I had a list of websites I wanted to research and punched in the first one. I found out that some sailors believed in superstitions and omens. To ignore a single sign could be dangerous, even disastrous. They studied the wind, the sky, and the waves. They believed you should never start sailing on a Friday. I wondered if Old Joe had been on a ship painted green or blue, because there were sailors who believed ships painted those colors would bring bad luck. It was unlucky if your ship was the same color as the water.

And rats? Gross. Mr. Jones had shown us an old black and white film on the big screen at the front of the classroom. The narrator practically shouted, "They were like rats deserting a sinking ship." And then the music grew louder, drums banged, and violins screeched. I used to wonder what it meant, and now I knew. Rats have some kind of super-sense and know when a ship is in danger. Seeing them leave is a bad sign.

I like numbers and discovering what they mean. In our culture, four is a sacred number. There are four directions: North, South, East and West; and four colors: yellow, black, white and red, one for each direction. Four is a good thing. For sailors, thirteen is unlucky. I found out you never want to set sail with a crew of thirteen because it would be unlucky. Ship launchings were very important. If anything went wrong during a launch, you were sure to have bad luck afterward. You never wanted to change the name of a ship because the ship might get mad and never forgive you.

Irish was sitting next to me and I nudged her after I read this.

"Look at this, the ship would get mad and never forgive you."

"Well, it's a good thing you're not a ship and you forgave me. Great personification, Cady."

Friends can surprise you now and then. Who knew Irish had been paying attention during English class and knew about personification? I didn't remember what it meant but I didn't want to let her know that.

"Um, yeah, it sure is," I told her. I grabbed a dictionary from the rack under my desk. I'm kind of old school, and like using a book dictionary because I like the feel of paper and discovering new words. I looked it its definition and found it meant "giving human characteristics to something which is inanimate." Weird, because it must mean the sailors believed a ship to be alive. They gave their ships names and called them "her" or "she."

"Ugh, history stuff," Irish muttered under her breath.

Just then Jeff started yelling and waving to the aide supervising us.

"Yes, Jeff," she replied. She walked over to stand behind him. "Oh, that," she added.

"Oh, that," Jeff yelled. "Look at this! Why didn't anyone tell us this before? Hey, we live in Upper Michigan and we're surrounded by the Great Lakes. There have been more than eight thousand shipwrecks on the Great Lakes, an average of one every eleven days, in the last two hundred and fifty years. Well, up until 2015. And only twenty ships went down from 1948 until 1975 and there hasn't been a major wreck since the Edmund Fitzgerald on November 10, 1975."

"Pretty interesting stuff, Jeff. Be sure to put it in your report," she told him.

Then the bell rang, telling us to move on to our next class. I was starting to get interested in learning about shipwrecks, but I still didn't know why this would be related to the mystery about Old Joe, the quillwork on the birchbark box, and the little journal. Did John Ray care about it for himself, for his grandfather, or for both of them? It mattered to me because I liked John Ray and I was learning to like solving mysteries. They were like puzzles. I'd always liked solving puzzles.

Grandma said she would help me: it gave me a good reason to call her and I hoped it would help me with my project for history class.

This was a lot to deal with and made me think of another new word I liked—*priority*. Francine, had taught me this new word. When you learn about *priorities* you learn which thing is more important than another thing.

"Cady, get your priorities straight. I've got my priorities straight, young lady. Family first and then work. When I'm at the doughnut shop I make a list of priorities—put the coffee on to brew, frost the doughnuts, wipe down the trays, straighten out the displays, keep everything nice and clean. I think it's time you started thinking about making some priorities in your life," she instructed me. "Tonight, your priorities are to wash the supper dishes and finish your homework."

I wondered if I'd made her mad at me because I'd forgotten to take out the garbage last night, and today had been garbage pick-up day. She gave me an extra piece of blueberry pie, so I knew she'd forgiven me. What were my priorities? I needed to think about this.

I finished eating my second piece of pie, using my spoon to scrape up the pie's fruit juice mixed with melted ice cream, when I remembered something that occurred earlier today. Gus drove the school bus to our corner, stopped the bus and opened the door. As I stepped off the bus, that noisy blue jay flew over it. His squawking sounded like, *"Priorities, priorities?"*

19 ⚹ Nishode (A Twin)

"Dad, can I call Grandma today?"

"Have you used up your minutes already?" he asked me.

"Uh, yeah, I've been talking to Grandma a whole bunch. I miss her, a lot."

"Well, I suppose there are worse things a teenager can do than talk to her grandma. I'll pay for another half hour and only half an hour. You can call her tonight."

I stood up to give him a hug and knocked over a glass of milk. Sometimes life was just so hard. I looked at Dad expecting another lecture and held my breath waiting for it. He laughed and said, "No use crying over spilled milk. Better clean it up."

The rest of the day dragged. I did my chores and went for a run. I even made a batch of chocolate chip cookies and only burned four of them! Francine made our usual Saturday night dinner: sloppy joes, frozen french fries and fruit cocktail. Not my favorite meal even if Colson enjoyed it. I dragged a french fry through the sloppy joe sauce when my dad looked at me and said, "Okay, okay, Cady. Once you do these dishes you can call Grandma."

* * *

My fingers shook a little when I punched in Grandma's number, because my grandma knew everything. Had she known Old Joe? Would she finally be willing to talk to me about him? Could she give me a hint or point me in the right direction to solve this mystery?

Grandma answered the phone after four rings.

"Cady? Hi, dear, so good to hear from you. I don't have much time to talk, so I'll make this brief. Why don't you come here for a short visit? Your dad is driving to Minneapolis soon to see Bruce, so he could drop you off here. Would you like to tag along and visit me?"

"That would be wonderful!" my voice practically exploded with happiness. Grandma is my favorite person in the whole world. I loved visits when I had her all to myself.

"Okay, I'll work out the details with your dad. *Bama pi, dear, bama pi.*"

* * *

The next two weeks passed in a blur. I had gotten serious about running when we moved here. I like running because I can feel the wind blowing through me, the wind is my friend. I love hearing it, either blowing softly or howling fiercely. I liked the *thwack, thwack* of my feet hitting the pavement. Even trying to catch my breath after a long run feels good. I've almost always run alone, and now I'm part of a team! Me, Cady Whirlwind Thunder, girl athlete, is a member of the school's soccer team!

A few weeks ago, when Dad and I told Francine that I'd made the team, I was surprised at how excited they both were.

I reminded Dad that practice times and games would cut into my babysitting time with Colson.

"Is that okay with the two of you?" I asked.

"Cady, you're my daughter, too, just like Colson is my son. The school year has just started; I'm proud of you for making the team. Keep your grades up, and we'll work something out. Oh, and keep working on your anger issues. I'd sure hate to see your anger get you kicked off the team. Learn to channel some of that anger into your sports, and it will become something positive in your life. Got it?"

"Uh, sort of," I told him. I didn't—although a little glimmer of what he said actually made sense. I knew I had "anger issues," and they'd usually gotten me into trouble. If I could channel my anger to help make me better at something I cared about, like soccer, then I'd try really hard.

My anger issues.

I'd been angry for a long time, probably most of my life. I think it started when Mom left when I was seven years old. I'm not sure where she went or what happened to her; I just knew she disappeared.

93

"Someday, when you're older, we'll talk about it," Dad said. Someday. Why did all the important stuff have to be put off until someday? Bruce had a different mother from me, so he wasn't any help. "Sorry, kid, I don't know the story. You have to ask Dad."

Francine and I weren't close. Even though she lived with us I still thought of her as my stepmonster, not stepmother. I wanted to cry because even though I lived with Dad and Francine and Colson, I still felt alone sometimes. It had been Dad and me for most of my life...until it wasn't. Change is just so hard.

* * *

The day finally arrived when I would see Grandma and not just talk to her on the phone. I could look at her face and sit in her kitchen and feel her love for me. I loved her kitchen. It's where my relatives had given me my woman's knife, and I'd learned to make applesauce and peach pie. Her big, old-fashioned farm-style kitchen had lots of counters and windows. It even had shelves (my grandma called them bread boards), which slide out from under the counters.

We left at 6 a.m. The fall days were starting to feel chilly, so I wore my fleece-lined denim jacket, an old pair of black faded jeans, and one of Bruce's vintage 70s band T-shirts. Dad had a thermos of coffee, I had two bottles of water, a cheese sandwich and some apples. I knew I'd have to listen to old-time country western songs on the radio, but I didn't mind because we were going to my grandma's. I planned to put on my headphones and listen to my own music.

After about three hours we stopped at a gas station.

"Pit stop, kiddo. I need to stretch these old legs of mine and gas up my pony."

Dad always called his truck his pony, which I secretly thought cute even if it was a bit lame. Grown-up humor he called it. I bought some chocolates while Dad paid for the gas.

Two hours later we pulled into Grandma's driveway. The truck's tires crunched the gravel, and Dad had barely stopped the truck when I spotted Grandma standing in her back yard. I threw open the door and ran into her open arms almost knocking her over.

"That's some welcome, Cady, but I'd like to stay upright if you don't mind." She brushed her arm across her eyes and started laughing.

"My, my, you've grown at least two inches since I last saw you. And, Ed, you're looking content and well fed."

"Now, Mom, don't start up with me," Dad answered back, but his smile told me everything was okay.

"Come on in, we'll have an early lunch, then you can be on your way. I think this girl and I have business together." An hour later Dad left with two blueberry pies for Bruce riding in the back seat of his truck.

* * *

Grandma made herself a cup of steaming raspberry tea. I poured my tea over ice. We settled next to each other on the couch in her living room. The couch's corduroy cover scratched a little when I first sat down but grew softer as I snuggled into it.

"Well, Cady. You want to learn about Old Joe. This is not a happy story, but it might help with your research for your class assignment. More importantly, it might help you and others to understand more about him and to not judge him unfairly.

"I told you Joe grew up in an orphanage. That was where he learned to fix engines, motors and other things. Did I tell you he had a twin brother? His name was Abe. They were fraternal twins, which means they didn't look alike. After they were born, the family kept Abe but not Joe. I'm not sure why. Maybe they couldn't take care of two babies at once. Who knows what their reasons were?

Old Joe was born with one leg shorter than the other. That's the reason he always walked with a little limp and how he earned his nickname, Old Joe.

"Once the two boys were old enough to realize they were twins, they tried to find each other. Things were different back then; we didn't have all this computer stuff and online searches. Most of us didn't even have telephones. The boys went to different schools and didn't meet one another until one day they were at the same basketball game. Joe was sitting in the bleachers watching the game when he heard one of the grown-ups point out a boy on the team.

"'See the guy over there? He's Abe, the star player. He's got a twin somewhere around here. I heard the family couldn't raise two, so they left him at the orphanage in town. Makes you wonder if they'll ever meet up.' Joe told us girls years later that was when he knew he'd found his twin.

"By this time Joe was sixteen years old. He'd run away from the orphanage and was living on his own in a little room in back of the old garage you asked me about. He helped out at the garage in exchange for a place to stay, his food and some spending money. The little room had a small cot, electricity and running water. There was a basic hose set-up to shower off, a sink, and a toilet. The garage was heated with a wood stove so the backroom was warm. Joe had to chop wood and haul it as part of his job."

Grandma stopped to take a sip of her tea. She set down the cup and looked at me and smiled a sad sort of smile.

"There's more to this story. A man named William owned the garage. William met Joe when he worked as a substitute janitor at the orphanage. His wife had died and he didn't have kids. Maybe that's why he helped Joe out as much as he did. He set up a little cook stove and hotplate for Joe and paid him enough so Joe could buy some groceries each week. Each year William planted a little garden behind the back of the garage where there were a few fruit trees so Joe had access to fresh vegetables and fruit.

"We didn't know Joe too well back then. Later he told us, William taught him a lot about fixing engines and motors. Joe was good at it, and he liked it. They worked together for a couple of years until William's cancer killed him. He left the garage and house to Joe. I expect he remained sad for a time because William had been the closest thing Joe had to family.

"A couple of churches in town offered free meals three or four nights a week, which helped. A few months later, Joe met Rose. She had agreed to help out at one of those church meals, and the two of them clicked the moment they met. It was love at first sight; like one of those good love stories you hear about."

I tapped my fingers on the table top.

"But, Grandma, what about his twin brother? I'm supposed to write a paper on shipwrecks. This doesn't sound like a shipwreck story, so how will it help my research?

"Cady, don't be so impatient. Try to sit still and listen."

Grandma raised her hand and waved it back and forth in front of her face. Right to left and then left to right. Right to left and then left to right. It was our secret signal, I needed to calm down. Then she looked at me—eye to eye, straight on. She gave me rules and expected me to follow them. It told me she loved me.

Grandma was my elder. I'd been taught at home and at school to respect our elders. They can teach us so much, not just about cooking and stuff but about other things like the Seven Grandfathers: Respect, Love, Honesty, Wisdom, Humility, Bravery, and Truth. We should have respect for our Elders and for each other. She taught me we should love Mother Earth and take care of her and that some things in life are sacred and shouldn't be abused. She taught me our Elders are here to guide us. Grandma taught me the Elders were our living books and teachers of our traditions, language, spirituality and culture.

"Joe's brother, Abe, didn't like book learning or school. He excelled at sports, and he liked the outdoors. He'd always loved the Great Lakes and signed up to be a sailor. People call them merchant marines or merchant sailors. He started shipping out on long trips. The work paid well and he got to see a lot of this part of the country. He liked the trips starting near Manistique and ending up as far away as Chicago.

"I've given you several clues just now telling you all of this. It's your job to put them together and solve the mystery. They will lead you to the answer. Have you started your research on the Christmas Tree Shipwreck? That story is part of the history of Old Joe."

"Yes, Grandma, a little bit."

"Just a little bit? Are you sure? Pinky promise?"

"Grandma, you know about pinky promises?" I couldn't help asking.

"Cady, who do you think taught you about them? Come on, your dad called, and he won't be here until early evening. I'm going to make soap out in the backyard. You can help me."

"Don't you mean soup? I thought you made soup in your kitchen."

"No, I mean soap...S—O—A—P. This is an old-time recipe. It's something my neighbor, Myrtle Jann, taught me to do. Ever since, I've always liked making soap."

"Like you enjoy making applesauce?"

"Yes, I enjoy doing it the same way I like making applesauce. Some of these traditions I've taught you are our native ways. Some are just things your old grandma likes to do because they bring back good memories of the past."

"Will I have those memories?"

"Yes, dear, one day you will have these memories. Not everything can be found in your computers. Some things we file away in the best computer ever made, our minds and our spirits, and call them up when we need them.

"Pay attention now, Cady. I like to follow the old ways. Myrtle did it this way, and she taught me. It makes me happy to know I'm passing it on to you."

I don't remember the recipe but it was relaxing watching Grandma and listening to her describe what she was doing.

After we had finished, we went indoors for more raspberry tea, sandwiches, and ginger cookies. Later, about 6 p.m., I heard Dad's truck in the driveway. Grandma hurried me out the door, handed Dad his dinner, and gave me a small package.

"Here's some extra cookies for you and a few bars of soap from last year's batch. Maybe you can show Francine how to use it when doing her housework and washing up the clothes. And remember what I told you about the shipwreck."

"Yes, ma'am."

"Looks like we've got company." I looked out the window and over her shoulder to where the sound originated. That noisy blue jay perched on a nearby branch.

"He's back," I shouted. "He's back."

"Yes, dear. Time for you to do more research," Grandma answered.

I heard *"Wheedleee, wheedle,"* with my ears. In my head I heard these words, *"Get to work, get to work, time is running out."* The bird's sounds were as loud and jeering as the words I heard inside of myself.

20 ⋆ Mitchimakinak (Mackinac Island)

Because the other schools in our soccer league are scattered all over the Michigan's Upper Peninsula, we often needed a few hours on the bus just to get to our away games. This weekend's game was different. The team would be traveling to Mackinac Island! Coach said we'd be going with both a male and female chaperone and twelve of us team members.

I told Irish about it after school when I saw her standing in front of school waiting for her bus to go home. I thought she'd be happy for me, but she didn't seem excited when I told her.

"What? Only twelve are going? What happens if more than one of you gets motion sick? Then you'd be playing with a smaller team on the field. Yikes, I'd hate to travel on a boat, but you go and have fun."

Why was she reacting like this?

"Gee, Irish, I thought you'd be more excited for me. I've never been on a big boat, or any boat, and we'll need to take a boat to get to the island. I've never ever been to Mackinac Island, people come from all over the world to visit there."

"It's just, well, I thought we'd hang out together this weekend. Now you'll be gone with those guys on the team, and I'll be left back here. I hate it. Hear me, Cady? I hate it!"

"We can do something on Sunday," I told her. "We're still best friends. I'll call you, okay?"

The assistant principal walked toward us, waving his arms.

"Girls, get going to wherever you need to be. Irish, your bus is leaving. Cady, you need to be at soccer practice. Now, scoot!" He made a big sweeping motion with his arms pushing the air behind us to get us to leave. At least he didn't yell at us.

After supper that night I told Dad and Francine I'd be traveling with the soccer team to Mackinac Island on Saturday morning. "First we'll take a school bus to St. Ignace, and then we'll take a boat ferry out to the island."

"Good for you, Cady. You should see the Island and learn about its history. As I recall, there's two ferry services to shuttle visitors to the island—Shepler's Ferry and the Star Line Ferry. Both depart from St. Ignace and Mackinaw City."

"I don't think we'll have much time to wander around. We're going to play a game. Then we'll probably eat somewhere and come back. Do you think I'll get seasick?"

He laughed, "I doubt it. You've never been one for motion sickness. I think you might like the ferry ride over to the Island. This will be good for your research paper. You can think about those guys on the big sailing ships, and try to feel how they did when on the open water. How is your research paper coming along?"

"Uh, it's coming," I replied. I crossed my fingers behind my back when I said it. I glanced at the calendar Dad had hung on the refrigerator and realized I had less than two weeks until I had to turn it in. I had to get a good grade on it, or I'd fail the class. Then I'd be kicked off the soccer team. Coach enforced strict rules and earning at least a C average was one of those rules.

"I'll have it done soon, Dad, I promise." My fingers were still crossed as I uttered those fateful words.

"Uh, Dad, what can you tell me about Mackinac Island?"

"It's an important site for us. Many of our people believe it to be the home of the Gitche Manitou, or the Great Spirit. It's well known for not allowing motorized vehicles on the island for more than a century. Most folks travel by foot, bicycle, or horse-drawn carriage."

He then handed me a brochure about the island.

"Look here, it states that the island covers a little more than four square miles in land area, is located in Lake Huron, at the eastern end of the Straits of Mackinac between Michigan's Upper and Lower Peninsulas. It was a long-time home to the Ottawa and other indigenous peoples before the Europeans came in the seventeenth century. It's now a National Historic Landmark. The

The Ottawa, Potawatomi, and Ojibway together formed the Three Fires Confederation. Anishinabe is the original name of the Three Fires before they separated.

"Native peoples believed the island's shape was like that of a turtle so they named it Big Turtle. *Mikinaa* is turtle and *Gitchie* is big. But now, Cady, I have a class to teach. I'm leaving, so you can use my computer to look up more information. Francine's home and playing with Colson. She'll be checking on you. Got it?"

He checked the time on his watch and raced out the door. I heard it slam behind him as Francine sat down and logged into the computer because I didn't know the password. She stood up and said, "You're good to go. You've got twenty minutes. Your dad said you could print out what you need for your report." She actually smiled at me and then started playing a game with Colson. I could hear the toy's beeps and bells ringing in the background as I read through the online information.

I learned that Mackinaw Island was controlled by the Americans, British, and Native Americans during different eras. It was the main hub of the fur trade in the Midwest.

I printed out the information and logged off. I'd need to study those pages when I was writing my report for my history class.

My dad was right. I didn't get motion sick. We won our game, and I even scored a goal— my first ever during a league game! Here's how it happened:

We were tied three-three at the game's end, which pushed us into a fifteen-minute overtime, and once again, neither team scored. This meant we had to go into a second fifteen-minute overtime, and members of each team lined up for penalty shots which is called a penalty shoot-out.

The Mackinac Island team and our team, Barnesville, took turns shooting at the goal from a penalty mark. The nervous-making part was that the opposing team's goalkeeper could block the shot. Each team chose five different players to kick the shot, one at a time, and teams alternated turns. A Mackinac Island player kicked, and then one of our team kicked. This happened four times until they had used up their five shots and hadn't scored.

We had one turn left, and it was my turn to kick. When I lined up to take the shot, I could feel the sweat forming down my back, but I told myself to block out everything around me and to focus. I could hear my dad telling me to use my anger in a good way. I channeled that energy into visualizing where I wanted the ball to go. I crossed my fingers, inhaled, and kicked. Then I closed my eyes for a few seconds until I heard my teammates yelling and felt their arms pounding me on the back. I had scored the winning goal!

We celebrated afterward with pizza and root beer on the island before taking the ferry back to St. Ignace where the school bus waited to take us home. I couldn't stop smiling the entire way back.

The lake was smooth during the ferry ride back, and you could almost smell and taste the water as the wind blew past our boat. I looked out on the horizon and thought about how the sailors must have felt during a storm. Coach told us we'd arrive on shore in about sixteen minutes.

I thought about the past and how sailors must have felt a hundred years ago when they were on the Great Lakes. They couldn't communicate with the people on shore or the Coast Guard if they ran into trouble. They only had themselves to depend on. Our ferry boat captain had ship-to-shore radio service, and almost everyone with me had a cell phone. We were traveling in early fall. I thought about how some of those ships in the past went out in late November and December when the waves could be high enough to cover the ship's deck and the wind would blow with fierce gusts.

I touched the little tobacco pouch in the pocket of my hoodie for reassurance. I was glad our trip across the lake would be a short one. This had been an adventure, exciting and fun, but now I just wanted to be back home.

* * *

Sometimes the other kids could be so silly. I mean it. We're supposed to be studying and learning about shipwrecks. It's a sad subject. I know these shipwrecks happened a long time ago, but people died and families lost their fathers and brothers and uncles. The kids I hung out with at school just wanted to talk about going on strike to change the school menu. Seriously? I wanted to shout at them. We had serious stuff to learn about even though I sort of agreed with them which is why at lunch one day I helped Irish to make a list of our favorite foods.

"I'm going to run for Student Council, and changing the school menu will be my platform? Do you know what a platform is?" she asked me.

"Of course, I know." I listened to my Dad and Bruce when they argued about politics. They were always talking about platforms.

"Yeah, it's something you stand on," Derek said and nudged Irish in the shoulder.

"Actually, Derek, you're sort of right. It's what I will stand on or stand for when I'm elected," Irish replied.

"Don't you mean if you're elected?" he responded.

"No, silly, when I'm elected." Then she smiled at him, and he got a happy look on his face. Before he left us he had volunteered to help Irish with her campaign!

It actually turned out to be kind of fun. We interviewed a lot of kids and made a list. Their favorite foods included: tacos, pizza, popcorn, jalapenos, cantaloupe, salmon, buffalo wings, oranges, ice cream, burritos, apples, steak, barbeque ribs, beef jerky, fry bread, cookies, brownies, fajitas and French fries. We made a list of the foods we didn't like. They were: onions, moldy pizza, snails, blue cheese, ravioli, old deer meat, frozen peas, pea soup, mushroom soup, soggy french fries, moldy apples, old milk and fried ice cream.

I'm not sure the other kids liked the same foods Irish insisted on listing. I guess we'd see what happened when she won, or as Irish told us over and over, "It's not if I win, it's when I win." The elections were one month away.

I fell asleep that night thinking about priorities. When I woke up, I had an idea. I'd go back to where John Ray and I had dug for the birchbark box. Irish was still apologizing to me for accusing me of stealing her backpack.

"Cady, you know I'd do anything for you," she'd told me. I was pretty certain she'd go with me if we went during daylight.

She called me the next morning. It was a Sunday, and she asked me to go to the beach with her.

"Come on, Cady, the guys might be there, and it will be fun. We need to have fun, don't we?"

"I'd rather go running," I answered. "Why don't you come with me?"

"You know I hate running, but I love hanging out at the beach!" I could hear her laughing and her laughter sounded like an excited dog barking.

"You could walk fast, and I could slow down. Instead of running I'd just walk fast and then we'd be walking really fast together. Come on, it will be fun." I hoped she didn't hear the pleading in my voice.

"Cady, sometimes you can just be so weird. Okay, I can stay with you for two hours until I have to get home to babysit."

We met at our favorite corner, and I punched her lightly in the arm. "I'll be line leader, okay?"

"Cady, line leader is for first graders," she drawled.

"I know, silly, come on. It will be fun."

I made myself move at a brisk walk, not too fast, because Irish wasn't exactly dressed for running or even walking. She wore red leggings, a pink T-shirt with gold hearts decorating the front, and a long pink sweater reaching to her knees. Her golden heart-shaped earrings were long enough to touch her shoulders, but it was her brown cowboy boots that slowed her down.

"I know, I know. I wore them because I thought they'd be easier to walk in than my pink fur-lined boots. I like to look stylish. Cady, where are we going? Because this looks a little familiar. We're not going to that yard in back of Old Joe's garage? I really don't want to go back there, especially without the guys. Once was enough." She slowed down, came to a sudden stop, and stamped her foot for emphasis. We were only two blocks from the house. We'd been so busy talking, Irish hadn't noticed our route.

"Come on, I left something last time. After I get it, we can leave."

"Five minutes, Cady, five minutes, and then we leave. Pinky promise?"

We each held out a small finger to seal the deal with a pinky promise before we walked up to the house.

"We need to go out back."

I grabbed her hand and led the way to the yard in back of the garage until we stood over the hole John Ray and I had dug. I breathed in. I could smell the mustiness of the dirt, a combination of aged moss, roots, and probably dead worms. I fingered the little leather pouch in the pocket of my hoodie. It was made of the softest buckskin and light tan in color. Bruce had beaded a butterfly on it using the tiniest of beads in shades of pink and yellow and blue. I had sketched the design for him, secretly hoping one day he'd bead this same butterfly design on my dance regalia.

Some people call our regalia a "costume," but it's not a costume! It's our regalia, it's clothing that represents our traditions and culture. You will often see us wearing it at pow wows because we want to look our best. In my family, we make our own regalia including the beadwork. I crossed my fingers and made a wish each night hoping Grandma would help me to make my own regalia one day. I knew deep down I'd have to wait until she said I was ready. Grandma would know the right time, and then she'd tell me.

I thought back to the day when I'd been here with John Ray. When we'd finished digging I'd taken the tobacco from the pouch using my left hand, and then transferred it to the open palm of my right hand. I'd bent down and scattered it over the hole we'd dug. We believed Mother Earth is living and has a heartbeat, and we should thank her for her blessings.

Both Irish and I were quiet for a few minutes until she broke the silence.

"Uh, Cady, what are we doing here? You said you forgot something, so where is it?"

I knelt down and moved the dirt a bit with my hand and pretended I found something.

"Here it is, I found it," I said and held up an old earring I'd put in my pocket before I left the house. I'd come to find more clues about the birchbark box with quillwork and its little journal. And I'd found it! Returning here and touching the earth had given me another clue. Not a clue that a person could touch but a clue that would help me to solve the mystery of Old Joe.

The day we'd dug in the dirt behind the abandoned house and garage John Ray had told me, "Remember, Cady, Mother Earth is precious." Recalling his words now made me think about water and the water that surrounded us in the Upper Peninsula. It was on those waters that so many shipwrecks had occurred. And, finally, Grandma had given me a clue by telling me that Old Joe and Abe were twins.

Now I needed to discover how these clues were related to the birchbark box and the journal it held.

One of the overhead branches swayed suddenly. The branch swung again and I glanced up in time to see the blue jay now perched there.

His squeaking noise made my head ache. Sometimes, that bird made me mad. I threw a punch in the air and hollered, "I'm not stupid."

"Who are you yelling at, Cady? I didn't call you stupid. Sometimes you can be so weird. Let's get out of here."

Irish turned around and headed toward the street. It was time to leave.

21 ⚡ Wawyeya (Circle)

I plunged into my research the next day with new energy. Dad checked on me almost every few hours asking me how my research was progressing and then making sure I kept up with my chores at home. And, I had soccer practice. Our last two games of the season would be played in the field behind school, so I didn't need to leave town. This left me lots of time for more research.

The facts I learned about the Christmas Tree Shipwreck were so sad. The ship's official name was the Rouse Simmons and Captain Herman Schuenemann had been in charge. The ship got its name because every year Captain Schuenemann sailed the Rouse Simmons to Thompson, Michigan, where she picked up a load of five thousand Christmas trees. The trees were stacked up in the ship's hold and on the deck. The ship and crew then sailed back to the docks in Chicago, Illinois, where they'd tie up, set up lights, and sell the trees to happy shoppers.

The ship left on a Friday, November 22, 1912. I thought about superstitions warning against sailing on a Friday and wondered if the captain had been in a hurry to get to Chicago with the Christmas trees. Because Barnesville was on Lake Michigan, I knew how rough the water could get. Dad had taken me down to our town's lighthouse last year during Thanksgiving week when a cold wind blew, creating the twenty-degree temperatures near the water. I'd worn my warmest parka, mittens, and fur lined boots just to walk from the car to the beach. I could feel the cold in my teeth. The waves made three-foot whitecaps on that day. I felt a little scared, and we were on land—not out on the water. I couldn't even think about how rough the water must have been that day in 1912 when The Rouse Simmons became trapped in the middle of a storm.

The reports I read said the boat was last seen during the afternoon of Saturday, November 23, 1912. She carried a heavy load, and was covered in ice, which can cause a ship to be top heavy because it adds weight. Ice is solid and sticks to railings and other parts on the ship exposed to the weather. Because it was fresh water blowing in a storm, it froze instantly.

"Holy cow," I murmured to myself. Did sailors have to chip away at the ice with tools just so they could sail the ship? My hands started to get cold and shake just thinking about it.

To calm myself, I started sketching a ship with ice on the deck and on the rails.

I read an account from a former merchant marine who described what happens during a storm.

"When you are dead in the water, you are at the mercy of the current. You're taking on water, and won't last long on the surface. You add weight to that, and you're going to sink. When boats are loaded with more than they can handle safely, you're going to sink. You can hope and pray, but you aren't going to last."

I did some more searching on the internet and found a website for the Rogers Street Fishing Village/Museum in Two Rivers, Wisconsin, which said the Christmas Tree Ship was seen by folks at the Kewaunee, Wisconsin, life station. Her flag was at half-mast, which means flying from only halfway up the pole. It's a sign of distress or trouble. The ship was heading south, and according to their website was "five or six miles southeast of Kewaunee heading south in a northwest gale. Then she was gone."

I cried when I read this, thinking of the brave men on board the ship who must have been scared. A search party went out when it was learned the ship had run into trouble. Searchers worked for two hours fighting against the weather, sleet, and snow, and ice. They had to head back in. They returned the next day but didn't find any survivors.

I tried to find out how many men had died. None of the reports could give an accurate account—maybe twelve or

109

seventeen or even twenty-three. And what about the trees on the ship? Some of them were later caught in the big fishing nets the commercial fishermen put out, others washed up on nearby shores for years and years. A scuba diver found the Rouse Simmons in 1971. She's now resting at the bottom of the lake, about 172 feet down, and she still holds some of the Christmas trees Captain Schuenemann wanted to bring to Chicago.

A few years after the Christmas Tree Ship sank, some fishermen "hauled up a wallet belonging to Captain Schuenemann," according to the Rogers Street Fishing Museum website. The wallet remained well preserved because it had been wrapped in oilskin. What?! Now I knew I was on to something. Could this be related to Old Joe's birchbark box and little journal? His journal was wrapped in oilskin too. I knew I had to look at Abe's journal once again. Maybe it would hold the clues to help me put all of this together.

I picked up my sketchbook and drew a lightning bolt. That was it! I'd write my journal assignment from the viewpoint of an artist traveling on the ship. I'd write as if I had been one of the sailors traveling on the Christmas Tree Ship.

I opened my sketchbook, picked up my favorite drawing pencil, and sketched for the next two hours. When I finished I had ripped the pages from my book and spread them on my bed. I'd drawn Christmas trees piled on top of one another, with waves covering the side of a ship. I'd drawn a view of part of a ship anchored at a dock. I'd drawn another sketch of a lifeboat. It was pushed aside, resting on the ship's top deck, and I made another sketch of a sailor holding a heavy rope.

I planned to paste these sketches into my journal and write a few paragraphs under each describing what I'd drawn. My opening pages would list the important facts about the Rouse Simmons. I'd describe its destination, date it set sail and what happened to it. I'd write the last few pages telling what it felt like to be an artist who wanted to sail the Great Lakes for adventure. I'd tell how excited I was and nervous at the same time and that

I'd wrap this journal of my voyage in oilskin for protection. I'd list my resources on the final page.

22 ⚡ Wigwas (Birchbark)

I was sitting cross-legged on my bed that evening when Dad knocked on the door and asked if he could come in.

"What have you got there?" he asked.

I showed him the birchbark box with its decorated quillwork. I held the little journal in the palm of my hand.

"Hmm," Dad hummed. "Birchbark is pretty interesting stuff. Legends tell us if you want to preserve something you should wrap it in birchbark and it won't decay. And if you look closely, you'll see the little marks on the bark look like little thunderbirds. Your little book was wrapped inside a birchbark box, so it's stayed in fairly good condition.

"Birch has quite a few medicinal uses. Did you know birch is a natural pain reliever because it contains salicylate, which is the compound found in aspirin? It can help with treating inflammation, pain and fever. It can be used to make tea to help with the pain of so many illnesses. And..."

"Dad, thanks, that's enough for now. It's great you think the marks on birchbark look like little thunderbirds and that birch can be used in medicine. What I want to know is why this box and journal were buried in Old Joe's backyard. Can you give me answer?"

"No, Cady, I can't. I've told you before, and your grandma has told you, this is your mystery to solve. It's time for lights out. Tomorrow is a school day."

I woke up thinking about something I heard a girl in my culture class say to one of her friends. The teacher had asked her the meaning of the word "*odan.*" She told him she didn't know it before adding, "I'm better on a different day."

"That's fine, that's okay. Remember, I expect you to be 'better' when you come to my class. I expect you to be prepared because you've made some effort to study. Got it?" Iris railed back at her. The girl looked at Iris and shook her head as if to say "Okay." It was up to each of us to show up prepared and to make some effort. I'd always liked to sketch and kept my combination sketchbook/journal in my backpack. I took it everywhere with me. I grabbed it from my backpack and started writing down what I'd learned in the past few days. Maybe writing it down would help me learn more, and at the very least, it would calm me down. I was trying to unravel this mystery. I could hear my dad telling me, "Well, Cady, trying is not doing. Do your best, girl, do your best and get going."

I picked up my favorite ballpoint pen, the one with the flower on top that lights up when I write, and started making notes.

What did I know so far about the mysterious birchbark box and journal?

John Ray, Irish and I had gone to an abandoned house that belonged to John Ray's family. We'd dug in the backyard, where we found this mysterious birchbark box containing a journal. The box and journal were decorated with a beautiful quillwork design. This same design appeared on my grandma's apron, and I'd also seen it at John Ray's grandma's house. When I asked both grandmothers about the design they changed the subject. Why was this so mysterious?

My Dad taught me a little about birchbark and quillwork and encouraged me to learn more about them and about shipwrecks. I asked myself how this design related to a shipwreck? And how was all of this related to John Ray's grandpa and his half-brother, Old Joe?

Wait a minute. If John Ray's grandpa was Old Joe's half-brother, then Old Joe's twin brother, Abe, was also a half-brother to John Ray's grandpa. Wow! I guess writing things down did help.

I opened the little journal once again. Abe had made entries for five voyages before his last one. He'd noted the name of the ship, the date they left, their point of departure, and arrival time. He'd described what they were carrying and how much it weighed. I rubbed my finger over the journal and noticed a small slip of paper hidden underneath its cover. Gently, I pulled it out, and as I did I heard that silly blue jay making a ruckus on the windowsill. Click, click, click went his beak against the glass as if he was tapping out, "Read, read, read."

Distracted, I accidentally dropped the piece of paper. It landed on the little table where I'd set a cup of ginger tea. Some of the tea had spilled onto the table top where it was wet enough to dampen the paper. Luckily, the moisture didn't ruin the words written on it which read: *The ink is there, but you must stare. The ink is blue, if you are true.*

What did those words mean? Was it a poem or another puzzle to answer on the way to solving the mystery of the birchbark box and its journal? I was being true to my gift, solving mysteries. Would that help me solve the meaning of the quillwork box and its journal?

I could almost hear Grandma answering, "No more excuses. Apply yourself, girl."

23 ⚹ Mzenakzegen (Picture)

The next two weeks passed quickly. Our soccer team ended up as league champions, which surprised everyone. To celebrate, the school board and tribal council were holding a banquet in the school gym. Trophies would be awarded to each of the team members and we could invite as many guests as we wanted. There was even going to be a giant sheet cake with pictures of each of us on it! Cake is one of my favorite foods and I love the frosting roses, whipped cream and icing.

Of course, Dad and Francine would be there. Even my baby brother would be included. I invited Bruce. He planned to drive here and bring grandma with him. Grandma had called Dad and asked to talk to me. She told me to save some time for her because she had something special to tell me. Bruce would stay with us, and Grandma would stay in the guest room at John Ray's grandparents' house.

The banquet was set for Friday night. I woke up to the sound of rain pounding on the roof. I pulled on an old pair of running pants, a T-shirt, and a waterproof parka. I ran to the bus stop, skipping breakfast because I'd overslept. I knew I could grab a banana or a protein bar and a carton of milk in the school cafeteria.

I had a hard time focusing in class. Our school had only joined the soccer league two years ago and now we were league champs! One of the kids had been called to the school office for something. I had overheard the secretaries talking to each other. He heard them say that awards would be given to individual players. This was big news in our little high school. Even Mr. Jones let us talk to each other during the second part of class, something he'd never allowed before.

Mr. Jones handed out the grades from our research projects during the first part of history class that day. I couldn't believe it,

I'd gotten an A-plus! Mr. Jones had drawn a smiley face next to the grade and wrote, "Congratulations, Cady. Well done. Tops in the class!"

I started smiling and couldn't stop. And then I thought back to last year and how scared I'd been, transferring to a new school and how angry I'd been about our move. I'd tried so hard not to be angry all the time and to behave myself and work hard. It actually seemed to be working. The rest of the day passed in a blur. The final bell of the day rang, and I grabbed my backpack and headed out to the bus for the ride home.

Gus, the bus driver, greeted me with a high five. What was happening?

"Good job, kiddo, good job. Now find your seat and let's get this bus headed to town."

* * *

Dad and Francine reminded me to wear "something nice" to the banquet.

"Maybe there's something in your room you could pull together? You never know," and then he winked at Francine who started giggling.

"Oh, Ed, you're such a kidder," she told him, which made Dad wink again. Gross.

I'd planned to wear my black jeans and one of the vintage T-shirts Bruce had given me. I went upstairs to change my clothes for the banquet. I'd been singing "Mary Had a Little Lamb" to Colson, and hummed the nursery tune on the way to my bedroom. I opened my bedroom door to a wonderful surprise. Spread out on my bed was a new pair of running pants, the one I'd been bugging Dad to buy me for the last three months. They were black with a red stripe down each leg. A matching long-sleeved black T-shirt with a red stripe running across the back was next to it. Black and red are our team's colors. I'd wear my new outfit with my favorite silver running shoes and my silver earrings. They were little bears, and Grandma had given them to me for my last birthday.

116

"You remember how to say bear in our language, Cady?"
she'd asked me.

"Yes, it's *mko*," I replied.

"Good girl, wear these and remember to respect what they
stand for," and then she'd handed me the little gray velvet box
containing the earrings.

"I've worn these for many years, and now I'm handing them
down to you." I don't know who smiled more that day, Grandma
or me.

* * *

The banquet was a feast. Roast beef and fried chicken, squash,
corn, fry bread and rolls, butter, a salad bar and even fresh honey
and jam! There was milk and cider for the kids and coffee and tea
for the adults. Three cakes were set out for dessert because there
were so many of us at the banquet. I counted twenty tables with
six or even eight people at each table. Little kids were running
around, and the adults were laughing and visiting. I looked
around the gym at the other kids on the soccer team and could
tell from their smiles and joking they knew our community was
proud of us for bringing honor to the school.

I'd even gotten an award for Most Improved Player. When
they called me up to accept the ribbon, I looked at Dad. He
smiled so hard you could see all his teeth. The best part was when
Grandma reached over and patted him on the arm and smiled at
him. It felt good to know they were proud of me because of the
recognition. I'd brought honor to our family.

* * *

Grandma kept her promise to me the next day.

"John Ray's grandma Eunice and I want to take you out for
lunch at Java Beans. We'll pick you up tomorrow at eleven
thirty," she told me as I left the banquet that evening.

That next day, after I showered, I put on my new outfit, the
one I'd worn the night before at the banquet. I walked through
the kitchen to get to the back door where I met Dad.

"Cady, time for your lunch date with the grandmas. Go on
with you and have a good time. You've earned it."

"Thanks, Dad," I said and raced down the steps and onto the driveway where the two grandmas were waiting for me.

That bird clock still hung on the wall in the coffee shop. The three of us were walking to a table in the back of the room when the blue jay started squawking the hour.

My grandma chuckled. "Cady, your buddy is welcoming you once again."

"Yes, Cady, that winged one is sure faithful to you. I'd say it's a good sign," Grandma Eunice echoed.

The two grandmas told me since I was their guest of honor I could order anything I wanted. I ordered a tuna fish sandwich, chips and ginger ale. I was still a growing teenager and hungry. I had skipped breakfast because Dad and Francine had let me sleep late. Both grandmas skipped dessert, but they encouraged me to order a piece of carrot cake. They sipped their tea, and after I drank a second glass of ginger ale. They looked at each other and then at me.

"Well, Cady, here is the surprise I told you about. Eunice and I agreed you should be told the story of the little birchbark box and journal you and her grandson, John Ray, dug from its hiding place. You've worked hard this fall, and we've decided to fill in the missing pieces for you.

"As you've figured out, Old Joe and his twin, Abe, were half-brothers to John Ray's grandpa. Abe and John Ray's grandpa grew up together on the rez. Old Joe grew up at the orphanage in town. When they were teenagers, Old Joe and Abe figured out they were brothers. They became close and would meet up whenever they could. Town is a good distance from the rez, almost twenty miles. Old Joe fixed cars, and now and then he borrowed someone's car to drive out there.

"Abe and Joe were restless guys. Joe liked fixing motors and liked to drive around. Abe liked the water and decided to work as a sailor on one of the many ships sailing the Great Lakes. Young and strong, he was happiest on the water and traveling. Once Joe and Rose were married, they were able to buy the abandoned house from Rose's relatives. I'm not sure where they got the money. They fixed it up and took in boarders and were happy. Rose loved to cook and garden," Grandma said.

"Oh, yes, and she was a talented artist," Grandma Eunice added.

"You're right, Eunice. She had quite a reputation as a quillwork artist. Collectors came from all over to buy her work, which probably helped to pay the bills. Oh, my, how she loved to create new designs! And she was so proud of her flower gardens. One year, to celebrate her spectacular flowers, she created a new quill work design. This is the design you saw on the birchbark box," Grandma added.

"And the design on your aprons?"

"Yes, it's the same design. Abe liked to keep track of his trips on the ships and recorded them in the little journal you found. He then buried it in the backyard of Joe's house where he knew it would be safe. Only Joe knew about this, and Joe later told my husband it was their twins' secret. They called it their buried treasure. If you look carefully, you'll see the names of each ship, the date Abe shipped out, and his port of destination. This is important. The last trip isn't correct because Abe switched places with a buddy. His friend wanted to stay home for his son's birthday celebration. Since Abe was a bachelor, he volunteered to switch places."

The two women looked at each other, and I wondered why they looked so sad.

"That was Abe's last voyage, he never came back. Like the Christmas Tree Ship of years ago, Abe's ship ran into a storm on Lake Superior and sunk. No one ever found Abe's body.

"Joe grieved his brother's death. This was the first time he cut his hair as a sign of his loss. The next year Rose died, and Joe cut his hair again. He stopped taking care of himself. Joe had the sugar disease—diabetes.

"People started calling him a drunk, but it wasn't that, he was suffering from his diabetes. He'd act strange and sometimes he wouldn't make sense. That was because of the diabetes.

"We tried helping him. We would take him to the doctor and keep him with us until his blood sugar was balanced. Once he was better, he'd return home, get back to work until something would remind him of Abe or Rose. He'd just shut down again and the whole thing would start all over again. It took a toll on his body. Diabetes, depression, they're both serious diseases and need to be treated. But unless one of us took him to the doctor he wouldn't go.

"He'd tell us 'I can doctor myself, thank you very much.' We did what we could, which was difficult because he kept to himself. He'd always been a loner, and he'd just lost too many people, first the nice man who'd taught him about motors and such, and then Abe, and then Rose. All of this became too much for him."

Grandma looked at me. She smiled a bit and reached out to touch my hand.

"Well, dear, now you know."

"Why was this made into such a mystery? And why did you want to me do this research? It doesn't sound like such a mystery because you knew the real story."

"When you put it that way, I suppose it's not," John Ray's grandma answered me.

"We know how people are and some people just like to gossip. We want the stories about Old Joe to be retold. He wasn't a drunk, rather he was someone who was grieving and ill."

"I guess I understand. But why was the house such a wreck?"

Grandma kicked me under the table.

I looked at Grandma Eunice and apologized.

"It's okay, Cady, the house wasn't always a wreck. Joe and Rose didn't have children, and after they both died, Rose's sister moved into the house and took it over. She took in boarders the same way Rose and Joe had. She kept to herself and didn't have much to do with us. It was only after she died that a lawyer contacted us and we found out John Ray's grandpa inherited it."

I brushed a tear away from my eye. I'd never liked crying in front of other people, even grandma, and I had to swallow hard and gulp a huge swallow of air to stop the tears I could feel pushing behind my eyes.

"What about the pattern both of you have on your aprons and other places? It's the same design on this birchbark box and on the cover of Abe's little journal?"

"Such a good question, Cady. Rose made two birchbark boxes with quillwork for her marriage to Joe, one for each of them. She made the little journal, with its quillwork cover, for Abe. She told us, 'This is my way of welcoming him into the family Joe and I want to make.' "She'd shared the design with Abe, and she'd only use it only for him, Joe, and herself. When Abe went missing in the shipwreck she changed her mind. On the one-year anniversary of his death, she gave each of us aprons with the same design.

"We wear those aprons on special occasions. She'd painted the design on each of our aprons and we're careful with them. She also gave John Ray's grandpa a T-shirt with that design on its front. She told us to never forget Abe, and each time we looked at her special design we'd remember him. Abe was so young when he died. He hadn't started a family yet, so it was up to us to keep his memory alive."

I looked down at the tabletop and then picked up my glass of ginger ale. I took another sip before looking at my grandma.

"Do you think Abe's ship was cursed?" I didn't want to sound superstitious but all the research I'd done made me wonder about things like this.

"No, Cady," Grandma said. She picked up one of the paper napkins on the table and wadded it in her hand. "It's just the peril of working on the water. Accidents happen and shipwrecks happen. I don't think superstitions control those."

Grandma always knew the right thing to say. Despite her answer, which made me feel better, I still had questions.

"Joe must have been so sad. He'd only known his brother for a few years, and then he lost him again."

"Yes, Cady, a real blow. At least he had Rose. The years went on and no babies came to them, so they started looking around to adopt or foster kids. Joe knew what it felt like to not have a loving home and wanted to provide a home for someone."

"But," Grandma Eunice added, "and isn't there always a 'but'? Then Rose got sick and died. Not long afterward Joe started to act strangely. He kept to himself, and hid from us when we stopped to visit. People stopped asking him to fix their cars because they stopped trusting him. All the talk about his supposed drinking started after that."

The two Grandmas looked at each other and shook their heads.

"We should have done better by him," Grandma Eunice said. "We should have known he wouldn't drink and that his diabetes was out of control. We thought he had a broken spirit from the loss of the two people who were closest to him in the whole world."

"We all should have done better, Eunice," my grandma said. "We were young then, raising our own families and just trying to survive. You're right, we should have done more."

I couldn't help asking, "Do you think a doctor could have helped?"

"Yes, Cady, but remember he didn't trust doctors. And after Rose passed he'd shout how much he didn't trust doctors. Rose was a wonderful cook, and even back then, cooked healthy foods like they try to get people to do today. She kept a big garden and grew all sorts of vegetables—onions, potatoes, corn, squash, beans and radishes, carrots, and zucchini. She liked to can these foods and put them aside for the winter.

"People often paid Joe with venison and chicken and even eggs. They ate healthy, which I think helped Joe a lot. Everything changed after Rose died." Grandma sighed. She stared at the coffee shop's door and seemed a million miles away lost in thought about the old days.

"Well, dear, have we answered your questions?"

"Yes, Grandma, all this makes me so sad. I wish I could help Old Joe but he's gone."

I looked up at the two grandmas. Grandma Eunice snapped her fingers and the bird clock announced the hour. It sounded like a blue jay!

"You can help him, Cady, and I'll tell you how. Isn't your school holding its annual talent show in two weeks?"

I wondered how she knew about the talent show. It seemed like she was one of those people who knew everything going on at the rez. My English class had made posters announcing the show and we'd put them up throughout the school, at the rez's administration building, in its vocational center, in the elders' residences, and even at the casino.

"I think I know where you're going with this, Eunice, and I like it," my grandma chimed in. She looked at me and winked.

"We'd like you to make a presentation during the talent show. We'd like you to show the birchbark box and Abe's journal and tell the story as we've told it to you. People need to know the story behind the story and put to rest those old stories. I think Joe would like that. Afterward, I'll talk to your principal and ask if the box and journal can be placed in the school's front display case. Behind glass and locked it should be safe. The children should see Rose's wonderful design and learn about a piece of their history. Yes, this is what you'll do!"

Grandma Eunice had this all planned out. Didn't she know I had trouble speaking in public? Asking me to speak in front of two hundred people frightened me. My hands started to shake just thinking about it.

My grandma noticed and reached out for both my hands.

"Cady, it will be okay. Eunice, the girl has trouble speaking in front of so many people. Being up on a stage would be nerve-wracking for many adults much less a young girl."

"Hmm, let me think about this. There's got to be a way! And it's better if the story come from a young person who's starting to gain a reputation for solving mysteries."

She stood up and snapped her fingers. "I've got it! This is how she'll do it."

She looked at me and said, "Here's the plan."

24 ⚡ Ekwak (The End)

The two grandmas told me I would be doing more than solving a mystery. I would be restoring honor to a man who deserved that recognition, and after they explained their plan to me I felt better.

"We will both be sitting in the front row and sending out positive thoughts to help you," my grandma said. She then handed me two index cards.

"I've written down the main points we think you should cover. These cards will help you to remember. It's best if you practice at home many times. This will help you to overcome your nervousness."

They made me feel I could do it. I could get up on a stage and speak to people.

Grandma Eunice had a photo of Old Joe and Rose on their wedding day and another one of Joe with his twin brother, Abe. She would have giant posters made from each of these photos and put them up on stage with me. She would ask her husband, John Ray's grandpa, to share the stage with me. During my portion of the presentation, I'd explain what John Ray and I had found when we went digging behind the abandoned house, and then I'd hold up the box and little journal.

John Ray's grandpa would then explain why this was important. He'd tell everyone his relationship to Old Joe and how, many years after his death, he'd inherited the house in town where Old Joe and Rose had lived. Because he'd had an operation on his hip, and couldn't walk very well, he'd asked his grandson, John Ray, to find the box and the journal. He told him where he thought he'd find it. John Ray had asked me to help him. He knew my reputation for solving mysteries, and since John Ray had to leave for North Dakota it would be up to me to solve this mystery. He'd tell the audience that I'd gotten help from the two grandmas.

And then he'd tell them about Old Joe and Joe's grief at the loss of Rose and his twin brother, Abe. He'd tell them Old Joe didn't have a drinking problem. He suffered from diabetes which he didn't try to control.

It sounded like a good plan, and I think the two grandmas liked it too because they smiled and clapped their hands.

"It's so good to put a wrong to right. Isn't it?" My grandma reached over to pat my hand. "This is a good example of a traditional teaching. We say that 'Your words are medicine. They can hurt or heal.'"

* * *

The sun blazed brightly on the day of the talent show. Grandma enjoyed herself visiting with friends in the elders' apartment building on the rez. She called Dad and told him how much she enjoyed meeting up with her old friends. She'd even been to the bingo hall and won two hundred dollars!

There was a lot of talk around the reservation about the school's talent show. It was turning into a big deal. I don't think any of the students paid much attention in class that morning. The teachers tried to keep us focused, but we were all pretty excited. Irish had trouble not talking in class on a boring day. All the excitement today inspired her to new levels so she kept poking me and whispering to tell me how great she would be on stage. She reminded me, again, that she had signed up to perform an Irish jig.

"I told you my clog dancing would come in handy some day and now it has. I'll be a sensation!" I hoped so.

Even though I was almost as excited as Irish, the morning dragged. I picked at my food during lunch (hamburger casserole with tater tots) and munched on some crackers to calm my stomach. Finally, at 1 p.m. the principal announced classes were over for the day.

"Students participating in the talent show are to proceed to the stage area in the gym. Other students are to report to their homerooms where they will wait until two p.m. when their teachers will take them to the gym," we heard blasted throughout the school.

My legs shook on the way to my locker. I dropped my books in and slammed the door harder than I intended.

Cady Whirlwind Thunder, you just calm down and focus. What you're about to do is a good thing and John Ray's grandpa will be there with you. It'll be fine, it'll be better than fine—it'll be great!

I used my favorite technique to calm myself, I pinched the webbed area between my thumb and index finger on my left hand.

One of the teachers lined us up backstage in the order of our appearance. A trio of sixth-grade girls would sing a song in our native language to open the event. They would be followed by one of the senior boys who would demonstrate how to take apart a computer and then put it back together. There were other acts: a freshman girl would perform a gymnastics routine and a sophomore boy pretended to be the Swedish Chef while showing how to cook soup; another boy played the guitar and a senior girl and her mother demonstrated how to make fry bread. A few of the kids sang solos and an eighth-grade boy wore his karate uniform and broke a board with his foot. Irish danced her jig routine. After she finished, the announcer congratulated her and added she would be the new Student Council president. Irish grinned from ear to ear while the audience applauded. Some kids even stamped their feet on the floor and whistled.

Then it was my turn.

I wiped my hands on my jeans (my favorite black pair) and walked on stage. Two easels had been set up with the large photos of Old Joe and Rose, and Abe. A student manning the spotlight shone its light on me. I stepped toward the microphone, cleared my throat, took a deep breath, and greeted everyone.

"*Boozoo* (hello)."

I said a few more words in Potawatomi just the way Dad had taught me. Then I held up the birchbark box and little book and showed them to the audience. I told them the story of how John

126

Ray had asked me to help him find it. I told them how Irish and I had helped him dig in back of the abandoned house. I then explained that inside the book Abe had recorded details of each of his voyages on the Great Lakes. He had written down the date of his last voyage and said he'd tell everyone about it when he returned.

After I was finished, John Ray's grandpa walked out on the stage. Because of his hip replacement he used a cane to help him walk. Most of its length was covered in bright red, green, blue, white, black and yellow beads. Beads formed a geometric pattern running down its length to the rubber tip at the cane's bottom. He had braided his long, gray hair, which hung down his back. He wore a pair of khaki pants and a beautiful shirt of black cotton with ribbons of red and yellow and white attached at each shoulder that flowed down the length of the shirt.

I looked at the soft brown shoes on his feet, and then I noticed his hands. They were beautiful hands with long fingers. The veins stood out on the tops of his palms, and he wore a heavy silver ring on the third finger of each hand. I stood a few feet away from him and noticed the turquoise stone set in one ring. I wondered if the other ring showed a bear paw design. John Ray had told me about that ring and how he hoped to inherit it one day.

"I have something important to say," he began in a surprisingly deep voice. People quit fussing and moving around and sat up straight. They shushed the little ones who were fidgeting until I could almost feel the eerie quiet in the room.

"This is a story which has long needed to be told. This is a story about three good persons who belonged to us and who have passed over."

He then told of the sad childhood of Old Joe, and how he had overcome so much to become a mechanic, how he had later met both his twin brother, Abe, and the woman he loved and married, Rose. He told of the tragic losses of both of these persons and how devastated Joe had become. He told the audience that Joe's behavior had changed because he was very ill and depressed.

"Listen to my words, that's why Joe acted the way he did, it wasn't because he was a drunk!" His voice grew so loud that people in the audience sat up straight and little kids quit squirming and wiggling.

"Joe was not an alcoholic. Sometimes we judge too quickly. Sometimes we don't help when we should, I am as guilty as anyone, and for that I am sorry. Words can be used to hurt or to heal. This time our words will be used to heal. These words can restore Joe's reputation, which I have done today with this girl's help and that of my grandson. An important part of this story belongs to Joe's twin brother, Abe. With the help of my grandson and his friend, we now have Abe's birchbark box and journal back in the family.

"Joe knew where they were and he'd told me many times that something valuable was buried in the yard behind his garage. The time was right to find them. They are both important pieces of our history. I'd like to display them in the school to remind our students that we are many things. I hope it reminds our young people that there are many opportunities open to them, both on land and on water.

"And now I have another announcement."

He paused until it seemed as if everyone in the audience took a huge breath at the same time. The air remained unnaturally quiet. We waited.

"The tribal council voted and has agreed to fund a group home for those young people who need a place to live. It will be named in honor of Joe and Rose and Abe. To get us started, I will donate their house in town. I wish it could be out here. Maybe in the future? For now, we will work with what we have. This is a proud day for all of us."

His speech was followed by silence. People looked at each other, then they smiled and started to clap their hands. A few minutes later the sound of applause filled the air.

25 ⚜ Bama Pi (Until We Next Meet)

"John Ray's grandpa was right about it being a proud day for all of us," Dad told me at dinner that night. "I'm proud of your contribution, Cady" he added. "We teased you about your clumsiness with a needle instead of appreciating your sketches. And now you have this new gift, the ability to solve mysteries."

I could feel my cheeks warm and start to tingle at this unexpected praise.

"Thanks," I said and stood up to get another glass of cider from the refrigerator.

"I just want to get back to normal," I told him. "I mean, I've still got the rest of the school year to finish. Soccer season is over, I actually received a high grade on my first big research project. Now I just want to watch movies and be with my friends and..."

"Yes, that's only normal. Another mystery will show up when the time is right so you don't have to go looking for it. That's the way we believe. Hold on, hold on, Cady, someone's at the back door. Will you see who's there?"

I crossed the hall and went into the kitchen. The inside door was open but the screen door was still closed. I looked through the screen to see John Ray.

"Hi, Cady, good job the other day," John Ray said in greeting. I don't know who had a bigger smile on their face, John Ray or me. He held up a package wrapped in white tissue paper. "Grandma said to give this to you."

Dad looked up from his meal and saw John Ray.

"Cady, where are your manners? Come on in, John Ray. Let's see what you've got there."

I unlocked the door and John Ray walked into the kitchen. He set the package down on the table. I looked at him, looked down and then walked to the table where I picked up the package. I tore off the wrapping paper to find a journal not much larger

129

than a postcard. Birchbark formed its cover, the quill design at its center matching the one on the birchbark box we had discovered. It was the same design decorating the front of the aprons the two grandmas both wore.

A note came with the gift. John Ray told me his grandfather had written it. "I recognize his handwriting." He looked at me and smiled, "Yeah, and he told me he'd written it!"

"Well done, Cady, I think Old Joe would want you to have this."

"My grandparents told me this needed to be with you now," John Ray added.

"Those old folks are full of surprises." My dad chuckled. "Looks like this is another one of Rose's works."

I noticed John Ray was looking at me again. This time I smiled back at him. He had a beautiful smile.

He could smile the sun into the sky.

"Walk with me outside, Cady?" John Ray asked.

"Sure, go outside with him. It's okay, I'll keep this fine gift here. You two go on," Dad told us.

* * *

We stood outside under an apple tree.

John Ray touched my shoulder playfully.

"I miss you, my friend."

"But you're here now," I replied.

Just then Dad stepped out onto the porch.

"Everything okay out there?" he asked.

"Yes, Dad," I replied before he turned and went back into the kitchen.

John Ray bent down and I hoped he would kiss me but instead he looked up to where that noisy blue jay perched on a branch of the apple tree brushing against the garage door.

He made a series of clicking and whining sounds before making a bunch of clicking and whirring sounds, "Wheedle, Wheedle."

In his sing-song bird talk I knew he was saying, *"Until next time, Cady. I'll be back."* He flapped his wings and flew above us.

I looked up at John Ray to see him smiling down at me.

"Until next time, Cady. Bama pi."

His words echoed those of the bird's.He walked down the driveway following the blue jay, turned and waved to me. "Bama pi," he said once again.

I had crossed the fingers on both my hands and whispered "bama pi" to him as he walked away. I had a feeling I'd see both him and the blue jay again.

Acknowledgments

"Cady and the Birchbark Box," is the second in the Cady Whirlwind Thunder mysteries. I wrote the first book after promising my students that I would write a book for them. I believe we teach by example and hope these books inspire them to use their own words to tell their own stories.

There are many I wish to thank for their help. They include but are not limited to:

- Linda, Gina, Amy, Evelyn and Christine for the many hours they spent reading drafts and for their encouragement.

- Haley Greenfeather English for her wonderful cover bringing Cady and John Ray to life.

- To Mare and Jenette for their help along the way.

- To bookstores of all kinds and our many splendid libraries. May they continue to encourage reading.

- To my publisher, Victor Volkman, for his support.

- To my family, students (past and present) and to readers everywhere.

Discussion Questions

1. Cady has anger issues and works to learn how to control her temper. Can you recommend some methods she can use?

2. Irish, Cady's best friend, ran for student council president. One of her campaign issues was to improve the school lunch menu? What kinds of food should she and her council recommend be included in the daily menus?

3. Cady is very close to her Grandma Winnie. John Ray is close to his Grandma Eunice. Do you have a relative (grandma, aunt, uncle, cousin, etc.) who has made a difference in your life?

4. When you are outdoors, do you ever look up and notice the birds? What do you see? What do you hear? What is your favorite bird?

5. Cady and John Ray find a very old birchbark box. Have you ever seen birchbark? How would you describe it?

6. The book told about shipwrecks on the Great Lakes. Where would you look to find out more information about this?

7. Have you ever had a mystery to solve? Did you solve it? Did you ask for others to help you?

8. Cady and John Ray found a small journal hidden inside a birchbark box which became an important part of the story. Can you remember a time when a journal, written by you or someone else, was important in your life?

9. Beadwork, quillwork, and working with birchbark are important parts of the Cady stories. Do you have a favorite craft? What is it and why do you like doing it?

10. Cady likes to run. She usually runs alone but sometimes with a friend. Soccer, however, is a team sport. What is the difference between a solo sport and a team sport?

11. Cady helped to restore the Old Joe's reputation to a place of honor. Can you think of a character in a movie, a book, whose reputation is restored and/or changed? Explain your answer.

12. Did you learn any new words this week? From the book?

13. Ask one of the characters three questions which need more than a yes or no answer.

About the Author

Ann Dallman has won numerous awards for her writing and has presented her work at national conferences. She graduated from the University of Wisconsin- Madison (Journalism Education) and received her MA from Viterbo University. A former teacher, she has written for *Marquette Monthly, Country, Farm and Ranch, Winds of Change, Chess Life, Salon Today,* and *American Salon* magazines, and the *Green Bay Press Gazette.* She was the writer and organizing force behind the book *Sam English: The Life, Times and Works of an Artist,* 2009 PEAK International Award winner, and compiled/edited *The Hannahville Poets.* She resides in Menominee, Michigan.

Contact information:
The author: lakemichiganpen@gmail.com
The cover artist: www.Haleygreenfeatherart.com

Photo Credit: TSG Photos, Marinette, WI

The adventure begins here!

Cady, a 13-year-old girl of Native American heritage, has experienced major changes in the past year-her father's marriage to a younger woman, a new baby brother, and a move from Minnesota to Michigan where she attends a reservation school for the first time. One school day, Cady finds an eagle feather on the floor outside a classroom and reports it to the principal. When thanking her for this act of honor, he tells her that a mystery might soon appear in her

life. Later, Cady discovers and antique Indian beaded necklace hidden under the floor of her bedroom closet. Is this the mystery the principal predicted might appear? She consults with elders who tell her it is her "job" to find out why. Helping her are her new friends Irish, John Ray and a talking blue jay.

"I was enthralled by the story, its interesting characters, the mystery plot, the author's beautiful writing style spiced with wisdom and humor, and what I learned about tribal cultures and customs."
— Christine DeSmet, author of *The Fudge Shop Mysteries*

"I LOVE IT. I could not put it down. I read the last few chapters slowly as possible the past few days because I was sad it was almost to the end of the book. I am looking forward to the next one."
— Faye DG Auginaush, from the White Earth Ojibwe in MN & Hannahville MI Potawatomi.

Learn more at www.AnnDallman.com

From Modern History Press www.ModernHistoryPress.com

CPSIA information can be obtained
at www.ICGtesting.com
Printed in the USA
JSHW040259250822
29583JS00001B/36